Enid Blyton's
MR PINK-WHISTLE
INTERFERES

"Where did you come from?" Paul asked. "You suddenly appeared!"

"Yes. I forgot I was invisible," said Pink-Whistle. "I didn't mean to give you quite such a shock. Let me have a look at that mack."

There was a big tear in it and a button was gone. It was in the goat, so there was no getting that back. But somehow Pink-Whistle managed to mend the mack. A new button seemed to grow in the right place, and the big tear pressed its edges together, gave a peculiar kind of squeak and disappeared.

"I say," said Paul, half-scared. "I say — you're a bit magic, aren't you?"

Also by Enid Blyton in Mammoth

Folk of the Faraway Tree
The Magic Faraway Tree
The Enchanted Wood
The Saucy Jane Family
The Seaside Family
The Hidey Hole
Snowball the Pony
The Adventures of Mr Pink-Whistle
Mr Pink-Whistle Interferes
Mr Meddle's Muddles
Mr Meddle's Mischief
Put 'Em Rights
Bimbo and Topsy
Those Dreadful Children
Amelia Jane Again!
Naughty Amelia Jane!
Family at Red Roofs

Enid Blyton's
MR PINK-WHISTLE
INTERFERES

MAMMOTH

First published by Newnes 1950
This edition published 1991 by Mammoth
an imprint of Mandarin Paperbacks
Michelin House, 81 Fulham Road, London SW3 6RB

Mandarin is an imprint of the Octopus Publishing Group,
a division of Reed International Books Limited

Text copyright © 1950 Darrell Waters Limited

Enid Blyton's signature is a Registered Trade Mark
of Darrell Waters Limited

ISBN 0 7497 0811 5

A CIP catalogue record for this title
is available from the British Library

Printed in Great Britain
by Cox and Wyman Limited, Reading, Berkshire

CONTENTS

I

MR. PINK-WHISTLE INTERFERES

I hope you remember dear old Pink-Whistle, the little man who is half a brownie, and has pointed ears? He can make himself invisible if he wants to, and he goes about the world trying to put wrong things right.

One day Mr. Pink-Whistle walked into the village of Little-Trees. There was a market there, and he wanted to buy some fish for Sooty, his cat. In the middle of the market were three stalls, and one man and his wife ran all of them.

One was for groceries, one was for fruit and vegetables, and the third one was for fish. Mr. Pink-Whistle looked at the man who was serving at the fish-stall, and he didn't much like what he saw.

"What a nasty-looking fellow!" thought Pink-Whistle. "What a toothy smile — and what horrid little eyes, set so close together that they're almost touching!

7

And his wife isn't much better."

He didn't think he wanted to go and buy anything from the fish-stall, but it seemed to be the only one there. So he went up to buy.

"Who's the man who runs these stalls?" he asked an old dame next to him.

"It's Tom Twisty and his wife," said the old woman. "Like name, like nature, I say! We never seem to get our proper weight of goods, or the right amount. But everyone's afraid of Tom Twisty. He owns half the houses in our village, and once he turned one of us out because we dared to complain about his goods."

Mr. Pink-Whistle watched Tom Twisty carefully. He was counting out some oranges for a little girl. "Let me see, you want twenty. Hold out your basket. That's right. Now — one, two, three — oh, that nearly rolled out, didn't it? Five, six, seven — wait a bit, that's a bad one — oh, no, it isn't — nine, ten, eleven, twelve — how's your mother to-day, dear? Better, I hope. Fifteen, sixteen, seventeen — will there

be enough room in the basket? Ah, yes—
nineteen, twenty!"

Well, I don't know if you have managed
to see how Tom Twisty cheated the little
girl out of five oranges, but he certainly
did. If you read his little speech again,
you will soon find out! She paid him for
twenty oranges and went off with only
fifteen in her basket!

Mr. Pink-Whistle was smart, and he saw
at once that Tom Twisty had cheated the

little girl. He stood still and watched, getting very angry indeed.

He saw Tom Twisty weigh out two pounds of flour, but Mr. Pink-Whistle was quite sure there were *not two* pounds there. He saw him empty eight pounds of potatoes into somebody's basket—but quite a pound of dirt went in with them too, and was paid for as potatoes. Dear, dear, dear—what a rogue Twisty was, to be sure!

Mr. Pink-Whistle went up for his fish. He asked for two pounds, and Tom Twisty's wife served him. She was not all smiles like her husband—she was a sulky-looking woman. She slapped the fish down in her scales, and although Mr. Pink-Whistle was sure that it did not weigh two pounds, down tipped the fish to one side, balancing the pound weights the other side.

"Is that really *two* pounds?" said Pink-Whistle. The woman glared at him.

"How dare you say I'm cheating you!" she cried in a shrill voice.

"I'm not saying that you are," said Pink-Whistle, in a mild sort of voice. "I just asked you if that was really *two* pounds? I want to know."

Mrs. Twisty picked up the fish and threw it straight at Mr. Pink-Whistle. It knocked his hat off. He picked up the fish, wrapped it in a bit of paper, paid for it, raised his hat, and went off without a word. Mrs. Twisty stared after him.

"I'll get the policeman here next time you come!" she yelled after him. "That I will. Accusing honest people of cheating! Ho, you wait till next time!"

Mr. Pink-Whistle slipped into a shop. The shopman was a friend of his and nodded to him. "May I use your scales for a moment?" asked Pink-Whistle politely, and popped his packet of fish on the scales there. He put a two-pound weight on the other side. Down it went, and Mr. Pink-Whistle stared solemnly.

"That fish can only weigh about a pound and a half," he said. "Yet I saw that it went down on the scales with a bump when it was weighed before—and I paid for two pounds."

"You've been to old Twisty's stalls!" said his friend. "He's a bad lot, and so is his wife. Cheating all the time. But he's rich and powerful and people are afraid to complain. They say he is friendly with the policeman too—pays him to keep away from the market when he's there with his stalls."

"Hum!" said Mr. Pink-Whistle. "Well, well! What a shame to cheat all the little girls and old women and busy housewives. I've a good mind to put this right."

"Don't you meddle with Twisty," said his friend. "He'll get the better of you. He's as sharp as a bagful of monkeys."

"Well, maybe I'm as sharp as *two* bags full," said Pink-Whistle, with one of his big grins. "Thank you for the use of your scales, friend. Good-bye."

Now Mr. Pink-Whistle was quite determined to look very closely at the scales and the weights on Tom Twisty's stall, so he went back in the dinner-hour and waited for Twisty and his wife to leave for a meal.

But they didn't. They sat and ate their dinner close by their stalls. Still, that didn't worry Pink-Whistle much. He decided to make himself invisible and do a little examining of the scales without being seen.

In a trice the little man had disappeared. He was quite invisible! He walked over to the three stalls and began to examine a pair of scales. He tipped them up, and saw that something was stuck to the underside of the scale into which the goods were tipped for weighing.

"Aha!" said Pink-Whistle to himself. "Oho! So this is another little trick — to stick something heavy under the scale-pan to make goods weigh more than they do! That is how my one and a half pounds of fish seemed to weigh *two* pounds. What horrid cheats!"

Tom Twisty and his wife heard the scales rattling a little and they looked up, wondering if anyone was meddling with them. But there was no one to be seen. Pink-Whistle was quite invisible, of course.

"Funny," said Twisty to his wife. "I quite thought I saw that scale-pan move."

"Nonsense," said his wife.

Pink-Whistle then took up the weights, and weighed them carefully in his hands. They seemed unusually light to him. Perhaps the Twistys used weights that were too light — so that they did not have to give so many apples, or so much sugar or butter! The cheats!

He took the weights over to another stall, belonging to a man called Bill Bonny. Bill had gone off to his dinner. Pink-Whistle popped one of Bill's pound weights into one side of the scales there, and put Twisty's into the other side. Down went Bill's weight with a bang, and up went Twisty's!

"Oho! So it's what I thought. Twisty is using weights that are much too light. His pound weight is not a pound weight and his half-pound weight only weighs about six ounces instead of eight. The rogue! He must have cheated scores of people all the time he has been here!"

He put back the weights beside Twisty's scales. Twisty heard a little noise and looked up, puzzled. But there was nothing to see, of course. Pink-Whistle looked into the sacks of potatoes. All of them had plenty of dirt as well as potatoes! Every little nasty trick that could be used to cheat people out of their goods was here.

"Time this was put right," said Pink-Whistle to himself. "High time! And I'll put it right too. I'll stand by Twisty's stall this afternoon, and give him a shock!"

So that afternoon, when people came to the market once more to buy, Mr. Pink-Whistle was standing close to Twisty at his stall. But nobody could see Pink-Whistle. He was still invisible! He was grinning to himself, because he knew he was going to have a good time. So was everyone, except Twisty and his wife.

A little boy came up with a bag. "Twelve grape-fruit, please," he said.

Twisty beamed all over his nasty face. He took up a grape-fruit and tossed it into the bag. "One — two — three — I say, that was a fine big one, wasn't it — I'll choose you another fat one — here it is — five — and another, six. . . ."

"Hey, you can't count!" boomed a voice right in Twisty's ear, making him jump violently. He wondered which of the crowd

16

round him was shouting like that, and was quite prepared to throw something at him. But he couldn't see anyone shouting.

"Count your grape-fruit, sonny," boomed Mr. Pink-Whistle, making Twisty jump again. "Have you got six?"

"No, five," said the little boy.

"Story-teller. I gave you six!" shouted Twisty.

"You gave him five!" yelled Pink-Whistle, putting his mouth close to Twisty's ear. "Begin again! And *I'll* count this time!"

Twisty was scared. He looked round for the man with the fierce voice, but he couldn't see him at all. The little boy tossed the grape-fruit on to the stall, grinning. Twisty, looking rather alarmed, began to count again.

"One, two, three" — but a voice boomed in his ear.

"I'M COUNTING THIS TIME!" And then the voice went on, as Twisty threw the grape-fruit one by one into the boy's bag. "One, two, three — isn't it a lovely

day—three, four, five—you're a nice little boy, you are! Four, five, six, seven—that was a nice fat one, wasn't it—seven, eight, nine, ten—did you say you wanted twelve? Ah, yes, nine, ten, eleven, twelve!"

Of course, you can quite well see that dear old Pink-Whistle was playing Twisty's trick the other way round, giving the little boy far more grape-fruit than he asked for, instead of less! Everyone began to shriek with laughter. Twisty was too frightened to say anything, and he meekly let the little boy pay him for twelve grape-fruit, when he really had eighteen.

"But I've got eighteen gr . . ." began the little boy in surprise.

"That's all right," said Mr. Pink-Whistle's voice, in Twisty's ear. "Twisty's pleased about that, aren't you, Twisty?"

Twisty wasn't. But he didn't dare to say so. Then someone went to Mrs. Twisty's stall, and asked for twelve pounds of potatoes. Pink-Whistle popped over to her at once.

He watched the masses of dirt going into the scales with the potatoes. Before Mrs. Twisty knew what was happening, Pink-Whistle had tipped up the sack and emptied quite half a dozen more pounds into the scales.

"Sorry there's so much dirt," said Pink-Whistle's booming voice, right in Mrs. Twisty's ear. "You shall have a few extra pounds of potatoes instead. Can't bear to cheat anyone, you know!"

Mrs. Twisty jumped. Where *did* that voice come from? And how did the potato sack suddenly tip itself up like that and empty more potatoes into the scales? She began to tremble. All the same, she wasn't going to let so many potatoes go! She picked out about six.

A sharp slap made her drop them into the pan. "Naughty, naughty!" said the voice. "Put a few more in for that."

And to Mrs. Twisty's horror, the sack of potatoes appeared to lift itself up and empty another score or so of potatoes into the big scale-pan!

Who had slapped her? She glared round at everyone, but there did not seem to be anyone near enough. All the people were laughing. What a joke! They didn't quite know what was happening, and most of them were feeling very puzzled, but all the same, how they were enjoying themselves! The Twistys were cheats — and now, for the first time, they were being punished well and truly in full view of the market! *What* a joke!

Mrs. Twisty said no more about potatoes. She turned away and pretended to be busy. Somebody went up to buy a pound of flour from Twisty. He slapped his pound weight on one side of the scale, and emptied flour into the other.

"*That's* not a pound!" said the Voice, from somewhere near his ear. "Here, put *this* weight on — it really does weigh a pound!"

And, to Twisty's horror, a pound weight was put into his scales, and his own weighed against it. Everyone cried out in scorn.

"Huh! Look at that! Twisty's weight has gone up and the other has gone down! Twisty's doesn't weigh a pound!"

Twisty began to shake at the knees. "Good people, it's a mistake," he stammered. "There's some trickery going on here. . . ."

"There certainly is," said the Voice, "and there has been trickery going on for a long time! Good people, tell Twisty to turn up his scale-pans! See what is underneath!"

Twisty tried to look fierce. He looked round for the man with the voice. Where *could* he be? "I'll slap your face hard!" cried Twisty, bravely.

"Go on, then!" mocked Pink-Whistle, and poked Twisty in the chest. "Slap me! Here I am!"

Twisty was terrified. He couldn't bear being punched by someone who wasn't there. The people roared at him.

"Lift up your scale-pans, Mr. and Mrs. Twisty! Lift up your scale-pans, and let us see underneath!"

Pink-Whistle lifted them up himself, and there, stuck underneath the pans into which goods were put to be weighed, were lumps of clay, flattened on to the pans to make them weigh more than they should.

Then the people went quite mad. They made for the sacks of potatoes and apples, they went for the sacks of flour and bags of pepper, they rushed at the slabs of fish—and before the two bad Twistys knew what was happening, they were being pelted with potatoes, apples, and fish, and having flour and pepper emptied all over them!

"You'll be sorry for this," sobbed Mrs. Twisty, "I'll turn you all out of your houses!"

"WHAT'S THAT?" boomed the Voice that the Twistys now feared more than anything. "Say that again!"

"No, no!" said Twisty, scared to death. "She didn't mean it. We're both sorry for all the wrong things we've done. People can help themselves to any of our market goods they please to-day!"

"And will you behave yourselves in future?" boomed the Voice.

"Yes, yes," said Twisty. "Certainly. No doubt about that."

The Twistys left the market in a hurry, and went home. The people helped themselves to all the goods on the stalls, laughing and chattering. Pink-Whistle laughed too, then made himself visible again and went after the Twistys.

When he got to their house he saw them coming out with their bags. They were off and away! They were too scared to stay in the village of Little-Trees any longer. They caught the first bus that came along, and Mr. Pink-Whistle got in with them. The bus would soon pass his own house, so that was very convenient for him.

The Twistys saw the little man opposite them and heard him humming a little tune. Mrs. Twisty suddenly noticed his pointed ears, and she nudged her husband.

"Look! That man's half a brownie. Look at his ears. Oh, Twisty — do you think he had anything to do with that upset at the market?"

Pink-Whistle saw them looking at him, and he grinned. Aha! The Twistys wouldn't play such tricks any more! They would be very, very careful in future.

He took out his packet of fish and sniffed at it. Then he looked at Twisty. "I bought this at the market to-day," he said, "and do you know, though it only weighs a pound and a half, the fellow who sold it to me said it weighed two pounds. And . . ."

But the Twistys had leapt out of the bus and gone. They had recognised that Voice. Oooooh! They were too scared to ride in the bus any longer. Where they went to nobody knows, and certainly nobody cares.

Pink-Whistle chuckled. "Another thing put right!" he said. "Won't old Sooty laugh when he hears *this* tale!"

And Sooty certainly did!

II

A WONDERFUL PARTY

Now one day Mr. Pink-Whistle met such a nice pair of children that he really had to stop and talk to them. The girl had a bright, smiling face, and the boy looked so strong and had such twinkling eyes that Mr. Pink-Whistle couldn't help smiling when he saw him.

"Hallo, hallo there!" said Mr. Pink-Whistle, looking at the two children. "Are you twins? You look exactly alike!"

"Yes, we're twins," said the boy. "We were born on the same day. Mollie will be eight on Thursday and so shall I."

"Ha! A birthday!" said Mr. Pink-Whistle, who loved presents and surprises. "I suppose you will be having a party?"

"Oh, of course," said Mollie. "Michael has chosen six boys and I have chosen six girls—so it will be a lovely big party; and do you know what Mike and I are going to have—a bran-tub! You see,

26

Grandpa has given us five shillings each for our birthday, and we thought it would be a lovely idea to spend it on presents for our guests."

"We shall put them in the bran-tub and everyone will draw one out!" said Michael, doing a little dance of joy on the pavement. "We're going to buy them now."

"Dear me, what nice children to think

of giving other people presents on their birthday," thought Mr. Pink-Whistle, who loved kind and generous people.

"Mother is making a big birthday-cake with both our names on," said Mollie. "It's going to have pink icing. She saved up the sugar icing specially for us. And she is making pink, yellow, and red jellies, and two big chocolate blanc-manges."

"And we are going to play Blind-Man's Buff and Nuts-in-May, and Postman's Knock, and all kinds of games," said Mike. "And there are six boxes of crackers — what do you think of that? Won't everyone enjoy themselves?"

Mr. Pink-Whistle walked along with the two happy children and watched them buy twelve lovely presents for their little friends. There was twopence over, and what do you think the children did with it?

"Let's buy twopenny-worth of those pretty pink sweets and give them to this kind little man," whispered Mollie. "I do like him!"

So, to Mr. Pink-Whistle's great surprise he was given a bag of bright pink sweets by Mollie and Mike!

"Dear me!" he said. "Dear me — how very sweet and kind of you! Just the sweets I like, too. Thank you very, very much indeed. I do hope you have a wonderful party on Thursday."

Mr. Pink-Whistle whispered magic words to himself when he went out of the shop, and disappeared. He wanted to follow the twins home and find out where they lived. He meant to give them a birthday present each.

So he trotted behind them, although they didn't know it, and saw the house they lived in. He wrote down the name of it in his notebook — *Fir-Tree House*.

When Thursday came, Mr. Pink-Whistle bought two merry birthday-cards, a big farmyard for Michael with all kinds of little animals in it, and a doll's house for Mollie, full of the tiniest furniture. Then he set off to *Fir-Tree House,* hoping that the children would be in so that he could wish them many happy returns of the day.

Their mother came to the door. Mr. Pink-Whistle raised his hat politely and asked to see Mollie and Michael.

"Well—have you had whooping-cough?" asked Mrs. Brown.

"Er—whooping-cough? What do you mean, exactly?" said Mr. Pink-Whistle, very puzzled.

"You see, both the children have got whooping-cough now," said Mrs. Brown. "The doctor came this morning and said they had caught it. It's such a pity, because it's their birthday, and they are *so* disappointed."

"Can't they have their party then?" asked Mr. Pink-Whistle.

"Oh no," said Mrs. Brown. "They might give other children their cough. They mustn't have others here for a long time. And, you know, they had got such nice presents for their guests, and I have made a lovely cake and jellies and things. I am really as much disappointed and sad as

Mollie and Mike are."

"Are they in bed?" said Mr. Pink-Whistle.

"No," said Mrs. Brown. "They are not ill, but they just have a nasty cough. They are in the nursery. If you've had whooping-cough, you can go in and see them."

"Oh, I've had whooping-cough all right," said Mr. Pink-Whistle. "I had it when I was five. Yes—I'll go and see the children, please."

So up into the big nursery he went — and, dear me, what sad children he found! Mollie wasn't smiling and Mike had quite lost his twinkle.

"Hallo, hallo!" said Pink-Whistle, bustling in. "Many happy returns of the day! My, I'm sorry you've got whooping-cough!"

"It's so dreadfully horrid of it to have happened on our *birth*day!" said Mollie, trying not to cry. "Why couldn't it have happened to-morrow? We've had our presents and our cards — but we can't have our friends here and let them share our cake and goodies and give them the lovely presents we bought. It doesn't seem fair, does it?"

"It doesn't, and it isn't," said Mr. Pink-Whistle sadly. "Can't you really have any of your friends to tea?"

"No — because, you see, not one of them has had whooping-cough," said Mike. "But perhaps *you* would like to come, if you've had it?"

32

"Oh, I should. I certainly should," said Mr. Pink-Whistle, beaming. "And do you know, I believe I could bring some guests who don't mind a scrap about whooping-cough — friends of my own, you know — very jolly ones. Would you like that? Then you could have a party after all."

"Ooooh — that would be fine," said the twins, smiling in delight. "Will you talk to Mother about it?"

So downstairs went Mr. Pink-Whistle, leaving the two big parcels he had brought for Mollie and Mike to undo. He told the children's mother what he had said to the children, and she nodded her head.

"I am sure that the friends of a kind little man like you would be nice to have," she said. "Bring twelve if you can, because I've got enough food for that number. I'll see you again at four o'clock, I hope."

Off scurried Mr. Pink-Whistle, back to his own little village. He burst in at his own tiny cottage, much to the surprise of Sooty, his big black cat.

"Sooty, Sooty!" cried Mr. Pink-Whistle. "We've got to find twelve people who have had whooping-cough or don't mind about it by four o'clock this afternoon. Will you help me?"

"Well, can't I be one?" asked Sooty at once. "I don't mind about whooping-cough at all. Would they mind a cat coming?"

"No — I think they'd be pleased," said Mr. Pink-Whistle. "I'll buy you a new blue party-bow. Now, come on — we must find some more people. What about little Mrs. Tickle? She's sweet. And dear Mr. Tiddley-Winks — I'm sure the twins would love him and his hat edged with tiddley-winks. Come on, Sooty!"

So off went the two to find more guests for the party. What a surprise for Mollie and Mike when they all arrived!

Now, when four o'clock came, you should have seen the twelve people that went trooping up the garden path of the children's house.

First there was Mr. Pink-Whistle

himself, of course, beaming all over his plump face, his green eyes shining. Behind him came Sooty, the cat, with a new blue party-bow tied very beautifully.

Then came Mrs. Tickle, a darling little person with such tiny feet that when she walked it seemed almost as if she was running by clockwork. There was Mr. Tiddley-Winks, a tall thin man whose hat was sewn with red, green, blue, and yellow tiddley-wink counters that jiggled and clattered as he walked.

That was four. The fifth person was the pixie, Tiptoe, who had tucked her wings inside her cloak so that no one in the street should see them. The sixth and seventh guests were two big sandy rabbits, looking rather shy but very pleased, each with a pink bow round his neck.

The eighth guest was a brownie whose beard was so long that he tied it round his waist when he walked, in case he tripped over it. The ninth and tenth were Mr. and Mrs. Roundy, who were just like their name; and the eleventh and twelfth were two goblin children, all dressed up in their best. They were not very pretty, for their noses turned up and they had such big ears — but they were so smiley that no one could help liking them.

Mrs. Brown was most astonished to see such a queer company — especially the cat and the rabbits — but she was too polite to say anything, and helped the goblin children off with their coats.

Well! When Mollie and Michael saw their strange guests trooping into the nursery, they were most excited and pleased. Gracious! What a marvellous party it would be, with rabbits and a cat, and goblin children and a pixie, and the rest.

Everyone had a present to give to Mollie and Michael, of course, though the rabbits only brought a bunch of early primroses each, which they thought were not very good presents—but the twins simply loved the pretty pale-yellow flowers, and Mollie put them into a little blue bowl at once, in the very middle of the birthday table.

You should have seen some of the presents that the guests gave to the children. Mr. and Mrs. Roundy gave them a dear little mug each, and as soon as it was lifted up to drink from, each mug played a tune. Mollie's played, "Sing a song of sixpence," and Mike's played "Humpty-Dumpty."

"I shall drink all day long now," said

Mike. "I think my mug must be magic."

Mr. Tiddley-Winks gave them a set of beautiful tiddley-winks each, of course, and Sooty, the cat, gave them a black china cat exactly like himself—and it mewed when its tail was pulled. So you can guess that it mewed all the afternoon, because somebody or other was always pulling its tail. It really was great fun.

Well, Mrs. Brown and the twins soon got used to such strange guests, and the party began. Goodness, it was fun to play Nuts-in-May with the rabbits and the cat, and Blind-Man's Buff with Mr. Pink-Whistle as the blind man. He kept catching Mrs. Roundy, who was a dreadful giggler and could never get out of the way in time.

The tea was gorgeous, because Mrs. Tickle had brought along a big tin of her best home-made biscuits, and as they were all made in the shape of toys, with jam right in the middle, they were most exciting.

Mike had a biscuit just like an engine, and when he squeezed it, the jam came out

38

of the funnel. Everyone thought it was wonderful.

Then they had the bran-tub—and how all the guests loved their presents! Sooty got a clock-work mouse, and when Mike wound it up and set it going Sooty was quite mad with delight, and chased the mouse under chairs and tables till Mrs. Brown felt quite giddy to watch him.

"I think this is the finest party anyone ever had," said Mollie happily. "Fancy finding twelve guests who don't mind about whooping-cough! I am sorry we couldn't have our proper friends — but I can't help thinking this is a more exciting party with this sort of guests, Mike."

Mr. Pink-Whistle was asked to do a little magic, because the twins knew now that he was half-magic.

So he was most obliging, and kept appearing and disappearing in a most surprising way. Mollie begged him to whisper the magic words in her ear, so that she could make herself disappear too — but she didn't get them quite right, and to everyone's great astonishment only her legs disappeared.

And there was Mollie running about the room without any legs that could be seen. Mrs. Roundy laughed till she cried.

Then they had the crackers. Sooty and the rabbits had never seen crackers before, and when the first one went off BANG, they were dreadfully frightened.

Sooty jumped up the chimney at once, and the two rabbits rushed under the sofa.

When Sooty came down at last, he was just as sooty as his name, and Mrs. Brown had to hold him under the tap and scrub him clean. Then he sat in front of the fire to be dried, whilst the two rabbits crept out from the sofa and wondered if they dared to pull a cracker themselves.

"Well, let's," said the bigger rabbit. "There are caps inside, Whiskers, dear — and you know I've always wanted some sort of hat to wear."

So they pulled a cracker, and then another, and out came a blue bonnet for Whiskers and a golden crown for Floppy. Goodness, they were pleased!

Then they played tiddley-winks — and you should have seen the way Mr. Tiddley-Winks played. He was simply marvellous. He could not only flip counters into the cup — but he could flip just anything.

"Flip this pencil," said Mike, and Mr. Tiddley-Winks flipped it — and it hopped

41

straight into the cup. Then he flipped the poker, and that went into the cup and stood itself quite upright. Then he flipped one of the little dolls out of the dolls' house, and she flipped into the cup and sat there, looking very comfortable.

"You *are* clever," said Mike. "I wish I could play tiddley-winks like that."

Then Mr. Pink-Whistle looked at his watch. "Dear me!" he said. "We must all go. We have to catch the bus. Good-bye, Mollie dear; good-bye, Mike. We've had a wonderful party, and we thank you very much for such a good time."

"Thank you for bringing such a lovely lot of guests," said the twins, and they kissed everyone good-bye — even Sooty, who was terribly proud of being hugged by the two children.

Then they all trooped off to catch a most peculiar yellow-and-purple bus that stopped outside. Mike and Mollie had never seen it before, so they thought it must be a special bus sent to fetch their strange guests. They waved good-bye to them and then looked at one another.

"Dear old Pink-Whistle," said Mollie. "Isn't he a darling! He's just the kindest fellow in all the world. When things seemed too horrid for words, he came along and put everything right. I wish I was like him."

"Good-bye, good-bye!" shouted Mike, waving to Mr. Pink-Whistle, who was the last one to get into the bus. "Take care of yourself, Mr. Pink-Whistle, and DO come and see us again!"

Good-bye! Good-bye!

III

A PUZZLE FOR THE JONES FAMILY

One afternoon, when Mr. Pink-Whistle was walking down a town street, trying to find a tea-shop where he could have a bun and a cup of coffee, he heard a mew coming from the small front garden of a house.

Mr. Pink-Whistle stopped at once. He knew that the mew was from a cat in need of help. Surely it couldn't have been caught in a trap? He opened the gate of the garden and went inside.

A tabby-cat was sitting on the front doorstep of the house mewing pitifully. She was thin and looked very lonely and miserable.

"Poor creature! Won't your family let you in?" said Mr. Pink-Whistle. "I'll ring the bell and tell them. And I'll tell them to give you a good meal, too. You look so thin!"

Mr. Pink-Whistle rang the bell loudly. Nobody came to the door. He knocked with the knocker, blim, blam, blim, blam! Nobody came. Then Pink-Whistle saw that the blinds were drawn down, and that the knocker wasn't cleaned, and that an old newspaper lay on the front-door mat.

"Why, they must be away!" he thought. And just as he thought that, a voice came from over the fence next door.

"Hi! It's no use knocking! The Jones family are away! They've been away two weeks, and are coming back to-morrow."

"Thank you," said Pink-Whistle, nodding to the boy who looked over the fence. Then he spoke to the cat. "And what have you been doing to get yourself so thin and miserable in two weeks, Tabby?"

"Well, my family went without leaving anywhere for me to sleep, and without arranging for any food for me," said Tabby mournfully. "I've had hardly anything for my dinner for two weeks, and though I've tried to catch a few mice, it is difficult, because there are hardly any round here. So I've got thin. But what has made me so miserable is that the family I love should treat me like this! It isn't fair."

"Indeed it isn't!" said Pink-Whistle in a rage. "What! This horrid family went away and left you all alone and uncared for! I won't have it! I'll go straight to the fish-shop and buy you some fish!"

So off went the angry little man, with the tabby-cat running at his heels, tail well up in the air. Pink-Whistle bought a fine bit of fish and took it back to the cat's garden. The tabby gobbled up the fish, uncooked as it was, and then began to wash itself, looking pleased and happy.

"Now look here, Tabby—I'm going to show that horrid family called Jones what it's like to have no food!" said Mr. Pink-Whistle fiercely. "You just wait till they come home to-morrow. I'll show them! I'll show them!"

The next day was Saturday. The family

were coming home after tea, and they had written to ask the milkman to send some milk, the baker to send some bread, the greengrocer to leave some potatoes, the butcher to leave some meat, and the grocer to leave butter, tea, and the rest of the things.

There was a little yard at the back, with a big box in which the tradespeople left their goods if there was no one to take them in at the back door. Each man left his goods in the box and shut down the lid. Mr. Pink-Whistle soon found out where the box was, because he made himself invisible and watched where the goods were put.

And then the sly little man opened the lid of the box, took out everything, popped them into an enormous bag he had brought, and ran off down the street. The tabby-cat watched him in amazement.

Pink-Whistle went to a row of poor old tumble-down cottages. In them lived three or four poor families whose children went barefoot. Pink-Whistle had a fine time there. Do you know what he did?

He opened each door of the row of cottages and popped inside the kitchen something that he had taken out of the box in the back-yard! Mrs. Tibbles got two loaves of bread. Goodness, wasn't she surprised to see the door open and the loaves hop into the kitchen! She couldn't see Pink-Whistle, of course, because he was quite invisible.

Mrs. Harris, next door, was peeling potatoes at the sink when she saw her door open and a bottle of milk and a large piece of meat come in. She squealed and dropped the potato-knife. But she soon got over her fright when she found that the milk and meat stayed on the floor, waiting to be picked up!

Everyone in the row got something. Then Pink-Whistle hurried off to the house again. The Jones family had just come back and were busy unpacking upstairs. The cat was mewing and purring round them, delighted to see the family again, although they had treated her so badly.

It was half-past six. Mrs. Jones went out into the yard to fetch in the food, meaning to get Mr. Jones, Joan Jones, and John Jones some supper. But there was nothing at all in the box. How angry she was!

She flew upstairs and said that Mr. Jones couldn't possibly have posted her cards to the tradesmen, asking them to send the goods. They quarrelled, and then at last John Jones was sent out to see what food he could get before the shops closed.

The dairy was shut, so he could get no milk. The baker had only one stale brown loaf left, and John bought that. He bought a string of sausages, some butter, some bacon, and some eggs. Then back he went home.

"Put them in the larder," called Mrs. Jones. "I'm just coming. Don't leave them on the table or the cat will get them, the greedy thing!"

The cat didn't get them — but someone else did!

Mr. Pink-Whistle, quite unseen, slipped into the kitchen and went to the larder. In a trice everything was under his arm, in his big bag! The little man slipped out again—and back to those poor cottages he went, chuckling away to himself.

And what a pleasant surprise the cottagers got again, when eggs, sausages, bread, and bacon, and butter suddenly appeared round their doors! They couldn't make it out. They ran to the door to see who had put the things there, but they could see no one. Mr. Pink-Whistle was invisible. All they heard was a deep chuckle from somewhere near by. It was very puzzling—but very nice!

Well, the Jones family were in a way when they found that the larder was empty. Not a thing was there!

"Did you put the things in the larder as I told you?" asked Mrs. Jones. John nodded.

"Of course I did," he said. "And shut the door, too. So the cat couldn't have got them."

"Well, the shops will all be shut now," said his mother. "We can't get any food for supper. Your father will have to run round to the dairy early to-morrow morning and get some eggs, milk, and butter. We can at least make some sort of breakfast then. And maybe the butcher has some meat over that he can let us have."

Well, Mr. Jones did manage to get some eggs, milk, and butter, and a loaf of bread from a neighbour in the morning. He put the loaf on the table, Mrs. Jones popped the eggs into a saucepan to boil, put the butter into a dish, and the milk into a jug.

But as soon as she turned her back, the things were gone! Yes—the eggs were whisked out of the saucepan, the loaf disappeared with the butter and milk, and when the Jones family came to breakfast, there wasn't anything for them to have at all! Mr. Pink-Whistle had been along again! Only the tabby knew what was happening, for, like most animals, she could see Mr. Pink-Whistle, even though he was invisible to human eyes.

There was such a wailing and crying when the children found there was no breakfast. "We had no supper yesterday — and now no breakfast to-day!" they wept. "What is happening? This is simply horrid."

The butcher let them have some meat although it was Sunday. Mr. Jones got a cabbage from the garden, and Mrs. Jones borrowed some flour from a neighbour to make a batter pudding. Everything was put on to cook. The joint sizzled in the oven, and the cabbage boiled in its saucepan. The pudding browned nicely by the meat.

"Goodness! I've never been so hungry in all my life!" said Joan. "I do hope dinner will be early!"

But gracious me, when Mrs. Jones went into the garden for a moment, Pink-Whistle slipped indoors, whipped the meat out of the oven, took the cabbage out of the saucepan, and popped the pudding into a dish he carried. Then off he went again to the row of tumble-down cottages. The people there really thought that they must have gone mad when a large, half-cooked joint appeared, a tender cabbage, and a big batter pudding!

But oh, the Jones family! What a way they were in! How they sobbed and cried, all except Mr. Jones who wondered what in the world could be happening. The tabby-cat sat and watched them.

"I'm so hungry," wept Joan. The tabby suddenly got up and went outside. She saw Pink-Whistle sitting on the wall and went up to him.

"Please, Mr. Pink-Whistle," she said, "don't punish my family any more. I can't bear it. They are all so hungry, and I know what it is to be hungry. I thought I would be pleased when I saw them getting as thin and miserable as I got when they were away. But I find that I am not pleased. I am only sorry."

"You are a good and kind little cat,"

said Pink-Whistle, jumping down from the wall. "I think you are right. We won't punish them any more. I will get them some food and speak a few words to them."

Pink-Whistle went to a tea-shop that was open and bought eight penny buns. He took them into the house and put the bag on the table. Everyone was most surprised to see the bag appear out of the air, because they couldn't see Pink-Whistle, of course.

"Look — what is it — how did it come — oh, who put that bag there?" cried the Jones family.

"I did!" said Pink-Whistle, making his voice very deep and solemn. "I am Pink-Whistle, your cat's good friend. You left her without food for two weeks — so I took away *your* food to make you feel what it was like to be hungry and not to have anything to eat. But your cat is sorry for you, and so I will not punish you any more. I have brought you something to eat. Look after your cat in future, or you will be VERY SORRY!"

There was a silence after this speech. It seemed to come out of the air, and was very strange to the Jones family. They stood or sat, their eyes wide open, wondering who was speaking. Then they opened the bag. There were only eight penny buns there — but, dear me, how pleased everyone was to see them!

And you will be glad to know that each of the Jones family felt ashamed of having left their poor cat without food or sleeping-place, and they gave her a bit of their buns. She is happy now, and always on the lookout for her good friend, Mr. Pink-Whistle. When she sees him coming she runs up to his legs, rubs against them, and purrs. And if he is invisible, it *does* look funny to *see* Tabby rubbing herself against nothing! You would laugh if you saw her!

IV

MR. PINK-WHISTLE AND THE BALLOON

There was once a little girl who loved balloons very much indeed. Her name was Susie, and whenever she went to a party, which was about once a year, she always hoped that she would be given a balloon, and sometimes she got her wish.

Now Susie very badly wanted a blue balloon. She had had a red one, and a yellow one, and a green one — but she had never had a blue one.

"I think blue balloons are the prettiest of all," said Susie. "I wish I could have a blue balloon on a long piece of string. I'd show it to all the other children."

Now one day a balloon-woman came to Susie's village. She was rather like a balloon herself, for she was round and fat, and her red shawl shone brightly. She carried behind her a great bunch of balloons to sell to the children. They were the

biggest and most beautiful that the boys and girls had ever seen.

Susie ran to look at them. The balloon-woman had a little stool with her, and she sat down on this at a corner. "Buy a balloon!" she kept shouting. "Buy a balloon!"

"How much are they?" asked Susie. "I've a penny at home."

"What, a penny for beautiful big balloons like these!" cried the balloon-woman. "No, no—these are threepence each, and well worth it, too."

"Oh—threepence!" said Susie, disappointed "That's very dear. But oh, look at that lovely blue one there! How I would like to have it!"

She stared at the blue balloon. It really was the biggest of the bunch, and it bobbed up and down as the breeze took it. Susie felt that she simply must have it.

"I must earn some money!" she thought. "If only I could get another two pennies. Then with my own penny I should have threepence, and that would be enough."

She walked down the road, thinking hard.

She passed Mrs. Jones in her garden, and Mrs. Jones called out to her.

"Susie! Whatever are you thinking about? You do look so solemn!"

"I'm thinking how I can earn two pennies," said Susie. "It's very difficult. I do so want to buy a blue balloon."

"Well, now I want a little job doing,"

said Mrs. Jones, "and I'm willing to give a penny for it. I want a parcel taken down to the post-office."

"Oh, I can do that for you," said Susie.

"It's a heavy parcel, and the post-office is a long way off," said Mrs. Jones. "You'd better see the parcel before you decide. I wanted my Jack to take it for me, but he's had to go to bed with a bad cold, and I can't leave him and take it myself."

Mrs. Jones showed Susie the parcel. It certainly was rather large. "But I can carry it all right," said Susie, "and I do so badly want the balloon that I'd be glad to take an even heavier parcel for you!"

The little girl set off to the post-office. The parcel certainly was heavy! It made her arms ache before she had gone very far. In fact, by the time she had almost reached the post-office, she had to stop and rest. She put the parcel down on a little wall, and hung her tired arms down.

And it was there that our old friend,

kind Mr. Pink-Whistle, met her. He was coming up the street, looking about him as usual, when he saw Susie.

"Hallo, little girl!" he said. "That seems a very heavy parcel to carry!"

"Well, it is rather," said Susie. "My arms ache a lot. But I'm having a rest now."

"Let me carry it the rest of the way for you," said Mr. Pink-Whistle.

"No, thank you," said Susie. "You see, I am earning a penny for taking it to the post-office, and if you carried it for me, it wouldn't be quite fair to get the penny."

"I see," said Mr. Pink-Whistle. "I am very pleased to meet a child who knows what is fair and what is not. Do you want the penny for anything special?"

"I do, rather," said Susie. "Have you seen the balloon-woman at the corner? Well, she has a most beautiful big blue balloon, and I am longing to buy it. I have never in my life had a blue balloon, you know. It costs threepence, and I am earning a penny towards it. I have a penny already, and when I earn another penny then I can buy the blue balloon."

The little girl picked up the parcel and went on again, smiling at Mr. Pink-Whistle. He went on his way, too, hoping that Susie would be able to buy what she wanted.

Susie was tired when she got back to Mrs. Jones. She was pleased to have a nice bright penny. She put it into her pocket and ran home.

She told her mother about the penny, and how much she wanted to earn another penny to buy the balloon.

"Well, Susie dear," said Mother, "if you want to earn a penny, you can turn out the hall-cupboard, and put it tidy for me."

Susie didn't like turning out cupboards, because spiders sometimes lived in cupboards, and she was afraid of them. Still, it would be lovely to earn the last penny towards the blue balloon!

So off she went to the hall-cupboard with a duster, a dustpan, and a brush. She emptied out all the boots and shoes, bats and balls, and the things that usually live in hall-cupboards, and then she swept the cupboard out well, and dusted it round. She put back all the things very neatly and tidily, felt glad there had been no spider, and called to her mother to come and see if she had done her job properly.

"That's very nice, Susie," said Mother. "Here is your penny. Now you can go and buy your blue balloon!"

Susie was excited. She took the two pennies she had and the penny Mrs. Jones had given her, and off she went to the balloon-woman. The big blue balloon was still there, floating at the top of the bunch! Lovely!

Susie gave the woman her three pennies, and went off with the glorious blue balloon. It really was very big indeed, and was exactly the colour of the sky in April, so you can guess what a pretty blue it was.

And just as she got round the corner, who should come along but Big Jim! Big Jim was a horrid boy, who loved to tease all the little children. Susie was afraid of him, because Big Jim often pulled her hair and pinched her.

She turned back, but Big Jim had seen her. He came running after her.

"Let's have a look at your balloon!" he shouted. "Let me hold the string."

Now Susie knew quite well that if she let Big Jim hold the string, he would go off with her lovely balloon and she would never see it again. So she held it very tightly, and shook her curly head.

"If you don't let me hold your balloon I'll burst it!" cried Big Jim. "Look — see this pin? Well, I'll stick it right into your balloon if you won't let me hold it!"

Susie held the string fast and began to run down the road. Big Jim ran after her and caught her. He made a jab at the balloon with the pin.

POP!

The balloon burst! Susie stared in horror. Instead of a marvellous blue balloon bobbing in the air there was now only a ragged bit of blue rubber on the ground. Susie burst into loud sobs. How she sobbed.

It is always a dreadful shock to any child when a balloon goes pop, but it was extra dreadful to Susie, because she had worked so hard to get the money for it. Big Jim gave a loud laugh and ran off. He thought he had played a fine joke on Susie.

Susie sobbed and sobbed. She really

felt as if her heart was broken. She didn't hear footsteps coming up close to her — but she suddenly felt an arm round her shoulder.

"What's the matter, my dear?" said a kind voice — and, lo and behold, it was Mr. Pink-Whistle again! He had heard the sound of crying, and come along to see what was the matter.

"Oh, it's my beautiful blue balloon!" wept Susie. "Big Jim burst it with a pin because I wouldn't let him hold it. And I worked so hard to get two pennies to buy it. And now it's gone. And the balloon-woman hasn't another blue balloon at all. It was the only one."

"It's a shame!" said Mr. Pink-Whistle fiercely. "It's not fair! I won't have it! Where does Big Jim live?"

"At the first house round the corner," wept Susie. "But even if you go and scold him, it won't bring back my balloon, will it?"

"You go home and cheer up," said Mr. Pink-Whistle. "I'll be along this evening with a surprise. Now, dry your eyes and smile. That's better! Good-bye!"

And off went Mr. Pink-Whistle to Big Jim's. My, what a surprise was coming to that bad boy!

Mr. Pink-Whistle looked very angry as he marched down the street. He turned the corner, and came to the first house there. That was where Big Jim lived. Mr. Pink-Whistle looked over the hedge.

He could hear a boy whistling in one of the rooms upstairs. That must be Big Jim. Pink-Whistle muttered a few strange words to himself — and in a trice he had disappeared! He was still there, of course, but nobody could see him except any of the fairy-folk.

Pink-Whistle went round the back way. The kitchen door was open, and he slipped inside. The cook was there, doing some washing up, but she didn't see Pink-Whistle, of course. He went into the hall and up the stairs, frightening the cat who had no idea that anybody was there — and yet she could hear footsteps!

Big Jim was in his bedroom, putting six big beautiful glass marbles away in their box. He was very proud indeed of those marbles. They were the nicest in the town, and all the boys at Jim's school loved them and wished they were theirs. But Jim was not going to give any away! Not he!

"Are you the bad boy that burst Susie's balloon?" asked Pink-Whistle in a deep voice just near to Big Jim's ear. The boy nearly jumped out of his skin.

"Oooooh!" he said in a fright, looking all round. But, of course, he could see no one at all.

"Did you hear what I SAID?" boomed Pink-Whistle. "I said, 'Are you the bad boy that burst Susie's balloon?'"

"I—I—I—did burst a b-b-b-b-balloon," stammered Big Jim in a fright. "It was an accident."

"That's not the TRUTH!" said Pink-Whistle angrily. "You did it on purpose."

"Who are you?" asked Big Jim. "And where are you? I can't see anybody. I'm

70

frightened."

"Good!" said Pink-Whistle. "Very good. You deserve to be frightened. Now — I'm going to make blue balloons out of something belonging to you! What have you got to give me?"

"Nothing," said Big Jim. "I haven't any balloons — or anything in the least like balloons."

"What were those things you were putting into a box?" asked Pink-Whistle, and he opened the lid of the marble-box. Inside lay the greeny-bluey-yellow glass marbles, winking and blinking in their box. "Ah — marbles! These will do nicely. You shall give me these."

"Indeed I shan't!" said Big Jim, snatching the box away as it rose into the air, lifted by Pink-Whistle's invisible hand. "Nobody shall have those. They are my own special best marbles, the finest in the town! Put them down!"

Well, Pink-Whistle was not going to be spoken to like that! He rapped his hand smartly on to Jim's, and the boy gave a yell and dropped the box of marbles. They rolled all over the floor.

"Pick them up and give them to me," ordered Pink-Whistle. Jim wouldn't. He just stood there, sulking to see his precious marbles scattered over the floor. And then suddenly an invisible hand did to him what he had often done to smaller boys and girls. His hair was sharply pulled!

"Ow!" said Big Jim. "Don't! Oh, if only I could get hold of you! Wouldn't I pull *your* hair!"

"Pick up those marbles!" ordered Pink-Whistle again, and his voice was so cold and angry that Big Jim found himself bending down and picking them all up. He put them back into the box.

Pink-Whistle, still invisible, took a piece of chalk from his pocket and drew a little circle on the floor. He put one of the marbles into it.

Then he muttered some words that sounded rather queer and frightening to Jim, and emptied a little blue powder over the big glass marble.

"Now, blow hard on your marble until I tell you to stop," commanded Pink-Whistle. "Go on. Kneel down and blow. Quick!"

Big Jim was so afraid of having his hair pulled again that he did as he was told. He knelt down and blew on the marble — and a very strange and peculiar thing happened! It began to blow up, just as a balloon does when breath is blown into it!

It changed from a round glass marble with yellow and green streaks in it, to a fine big yellow-green balloon. Marvellous!

"Oooh, that's funny," said Big Jim. "My glass marble has changed into a balloon. I shall like taking that about with me."

"It's not for you," said Pink-Whistle, taking the balloon out of the circle and quickly tying a piece of string on to it. "It's for Susie. Now here's the next one. Blue, please!"

Mr. Pink-Whistle put a blue-green marble into the circle of chalk and once again Big Jim had to blow. How he blew! He didn't want to, but he was really afraid of the person he couldn't see but could only hear and feel!

That marble blew up into a balloon too — a fine bluey-green one that Pink-Whistle quickly tied up with another piece of string.

Then into the circle went the third marble. "Oh, I say," said Big Jim. "I'm not going to have any more of my beautiful glass marbles changed into balloons.

I just won't have it!"

A hard hand came out and caught hold of Jim's right ear, just in the same way that Jim had so often taken hold of other people's ears! His head was pulled towards the circle, and he had to blow! He blew and he blew. That marble was very hard to blow up, but Pink-Whistle didn't leave go his hold on Jim's ear until the balloon was really quite enormous.

Well, Big Jim had to blow all his precious marbles into balloons! Soon there were six fine balloons waving in the bedroom on the end of strings—and the box of marbles was empty!

"Thank you," said Pink-Whistle, taking all the strings into one hand, "Susie shall have all these. I am sure she will especially love this big blue one made out of your best blue marble, because it is almost exactly the colour of the one you burst. Well, good-bye."

"Don't take those balloons to Susie," said Big Jim with tears in his eyes. "You know quite well they are really my marbles that you've changed by some magic. Please, please, don't take them."

"How many times have children said, 'Please, please,' to you, Big Jim, when you have been unkind to them?" asked Pink-Whistle. "Did you take any notice? No, you didn't. Well, neither shall I. You needed a lesson, my boy, and you've had it. Learn from it and it won't be wasted. You have had to give up something you really loved yourself in order to make up for robbing someone else of something they loved. Remember what it feels like, and be kinder in future!"

Off went the little brownie-man, taking the string of balloons with him. He met Jim's mother in the hall, and she was most amazed and astonished to see a string of balloons going through the hall by themselves—for she couldn't see anyone holding them, of course!

"Pardon me, Madam!" said Pink-Whistle politely, forgetting that he was invisible.

"Oh! Gracious me—talking balloons!" cried Jim's mother, and fled into the kitchen. Pink-Whistle chuckled, and went out of the front door. He trotted along to Susie, first making himself seen, because he knew that people would be most astonished to see balloons floating down the street by themselves.

He came to Susie's house. Susie was in the front garden. Her eyes were red, and she looked sad. When she saw Pink-

Whistle coming along with a whole bunch of balloons, she gave a squeal of delight.

"Oh! What marvellous balloons! Oh, where did you get that wonderful blue one from? It's even bigger than the one Big Jim burst!"

"I got these from Big Jim," said Pink-Whistle. "I made them from his precious marbles! They are stronger than ordinary balloons, my dear. Take them and enjoy them!"

Susie took the strings, going red with surprise and delight. "Oh!" she said, "I shall give a tea-party, and let each of my guests have a balloon to take home."

"Well, the big blue one is especially yours," said Pink-Whistle. "Be sure you keep that!"

So Susie did, of course, and she still has it hanging in her bedroom. She gave the others away at a party, and how the children loved them! Wouldn't it be nice if Pink-Whistle came along when any of *our* balloons went POP? Well—you never know!

V

MR. PINK-WHISTLE'S CIRCUS

There was once a little girl called Eileen, who was feeling very excited because she had been asked to go to the circus.

Her friend was going with her mother, and they asked Eileen to go, too. So she was very happy, and she counted the days till the Great Day came.

"Mother, it's Galliano's Circus," she said happily. "I shall see Lotta on her horse, Black Beauty, and I shall see Jimmy and his performing dog, Lucky. I shall see Jumbo, the dear old elephant, playing cricket with his keeper, and I shall see Lilliput and all his monkeys. Oh, won't it be fun?"

The day came at last. Eileen woke up—but oh, what a pity, she had a horrid sore feeling in her throat that made her choke and cough. Mother heard her and came in.

"Have you got a sore throat?" she asked

Eileen. The little girl didn't want to say yes, because she knew that sore throats meant being kept in bed — but she always told her mother the truth, so she nodded her head.

"It's not very bad, Mother," she said. "It won't stop my going to the circus. I can hardly feel it."

Then she coughed again, and that hurt her throat. Mother made her open her mouth.

"Oh, darling," she said, "you really have got a very nasty throat. I simply daren't let you go out to-day. And, besides, Mary might catch it if you go with her. You can't possibly go out — you must stay in bed."

Poor Eileen. She began to cry bitterly, and buried her face in her pillow. "It's not fair," she wept. "Just the very day I was going to the circus — the VERY day! Oh, I do feel so unhappy. Now Mary will go without me. They will take someone else. Somebody else will have my treat. Mother, it's NOT FAIR."

"No—it doesn't seem fair, darling," said Mother. "But things aren't always fair, you know. Cheer up. I will go out and buy you a toy this afternoon when you sleep. Then you shall have it at tea-time."

Mother went out of the room. Eileen cried for a little while, then she fell asleep. She didn't want any breakfast, and she didn't want any dinner. Her throat hurt her. She was cross and miserable.

When Mother tucked her up for an afternoon rest, Eileen began to sob again.

"Mary and her mother are just starting out for the circus. They're catching the bus. Mother, it isn't fair!"

"Now don't cry any more or you won't sleep," said Mother, and she went to the door. "I'm just going out to buy you a surprise."

Eileen heard the front door bang. She tried to go to sleep, but she couldn't. She kept thinking of Mary. Now they would have arrived at the circus. Now they would be taking their seats round the ring. Now the band would play.

She began to cry again. She wasn't really a cry-baby, but when you feel ill you can't help crying at all kinds of things, can you?

"I don't think it's a bit fair," wept the little girl. "I don't, I don't."

Now who should come along under the window at that very minute but dear old Mr. Pink-Whistle! You know how he loves to put things right, if he can—so you can guess that he stopped at once and listened.

"A little girl in trouble!" he said to himself. "I must look into this!"

He went to the front door and pushed it. It opened to him, for he was half-magic. Up the stairs he went and into Eileen's room. The little girl heard him opening the door, and she stared at him in surprise, for he had the green eyes and pointed ears of the fairy-folk.

"Hallo," said Mr. Pink-Whistle. "What's the trouble?"

"I was going to the circus to-day—but now I've got a bad throat and I can't," said Eileen, the tears running down her cheeks again. "Who are you? I like you."

"I'm Mr. Pink-Whistle," said the little man. "I like you, too. I think you would be quite pretty if you didn't spoil your face with crying."

"Well, you'd cry, too, if you couldn't go to the circus after all," said Eileen. "I just simply can't help it. I keep thinking of it."

"I suppose you wouldn't like to see my circus, would you?" suddenly asked Mr. Pink-Whistle. "I mean I'm sure it isn't as good as Galliano's—but it's quite fun."

"But how can I see it if I'm in bed?" said Eileen in astonishment.

"Easily!" said Pink-Whistle. "There's room on your bed for my circus to perform. Do you mind putting your legs down flat? That's right. Now look—this is the ring—and you are the people looking on,

84

so you must clap when anything good is done."

"But where's the circus?" asked Eileen.

"Just a minute, just a minute," said Mr. Pink-Whistle, and he ran into the room next door, which was Eileen's nursery. There were plenty of toys there and it didn't take Pink-Whistle long to rub a little magic on to the ones he wanted for his circus! His magic made them all come alive, and in half a minute he had told them all what to do. Then he went back into the bedroom.

"The circus is coming!" he said. "Listen to the band!"

In came the band! It was the baby doll carrying the musical box, playing a merry tune by turning the handle round and round — and the pink cat playing the little drum in time to the tune — rum-ti-tum-ti-tum, tum-ti-tum-ti-tum! They climbed up on to the bed and settled down to play their little band together. Eileen was so surprised!

Then in came the toy elephant, Jumbo,

led by his keeper, one of the boy-dolls! They climbed up on to the bed, too, and to Eileen's great joy they played cricket together just like the real Jumbo and his keeper at the big circus. Her toy elephant was very clever at hitting the ball that the doll threw to him, and once he hit it so hard that it bounced on Mr. Pink-Whistle's nose with a loud "ping"!

That made everyone laugh. Eileen clapped loudly. "Now come the next performers," said Pink-Whistle. The band struck up a merry tune again, and rum-ti-tum-ti-tum went the drum. In came the sailor doll with all the teddy bears tied together in a row.

"The performing bears!" said Pink-Whistle. "Play up, band — the bears want to dance!"

Well, those teddy bears did dance! They danced all over the bed, they rolled about, they grunted and growled, and they had just as good a time as Eileen herself had.

"Well, I'd no idea my bears could be so funny, Mr. Pink-Whistle!" she said. "If

I laugh much more I'll get a stitch in my side."

Then in galloped the little brown horse without the wooden cart it usually pulled along. Riding on its back was the fairy doll! She did look simply lovely, and Eileen was most surprised to see how clever she was! She stood up on the horse's back, and galloped over the bed like that. Then she stood on one leg only and didn't fall off once.

"Marvellous!" said Eileen. "Oh, Mr. Pink-Whistle, this is simply lovely. What's next?"

"Your two monkeys come next," said the little man. "Here they are."

And in they came, grinning all over their faces. What a time they had! They didn't stay on the bed. They leapt all over the room, and swung by their tails from the lamp that hung down from the ceiling. They climbed all over Pink-Whistle, and when he took some bananas from his pocket and gave them to the monkeys, they peeled them neatly and gobbled them up.

"Aren't they clever?" said Eileen. "Oh, Mr. Pink-Whistle, I think I'd rather see your circus than even Mr. Galliano's — because, you see, your circus is made of all my own toys, and I really didn't know they were so clever. Oh, look — here come all my toy soldiers on horse-back!"

The soldiers galloped in. The band struck up again — and hey presto, all those horses began to dance prettily round the bed in time to the music—just like the horses do in any circus. It was marvellous to watch. Suddenly the front door opened. It was Mother back from her walk. Eileen stared at Mr. Pink-Whistle.

"That's mother!" she said. "I wonder what she's brought me. Oh, Mr. Pink-Whistle, do stay and let her see the circus, too."

"Sorry, little girl, I can't," said Pink-Whistle. "I don't want your mother to see me. I'm going to disappear and slip down the stairs. Watch me!"

Eileen watched him—and to her very great amazement the merry little man seemed to dissolve like sugar in a cup—and then he wasn't there at all! But his voice came to her from near the door.

"Good-bye. So glad you liked my circus. Do things seem a bit fairer now?"

"Oh yes!" cried Eileen. And then down the stairs went Pink-Whistle, opened the front door, and was gone. Mother saw the front door opening and shutting by itself and she was most surprised. You see, she couldn't see Pink-Whistle at all.

She went up the stairs—and as soon as she came to Eileen's door, an extraordinary thing happened. All the toys had hopped down from Eileen's bed and were running back to the nursery. There they went—monkeys, dolls, bears, and all. Mother simply couldn't believe her eyes.

"I must be imagining things," she thought. She peeped into the nursery. All the toys were in their places, as still as could be. Nobody could ever imagine they had been in Mr. Pink-Whistle's circus all afternoon. "Eileen! What do you think I've bought you?" cried Mother, going into the bedroom. "Look—a little toy circus! Won't you love that?"

"Yes, I will," said Eileen, sitting up joyfully. "But, Mother—I shall always like Mr. Pink-Whistle's circus the very best of all!"

And I'm sure I would, too, wouldn't you?

VI

MR. PINK-WHISTLE AND THE COWARDS

Paul went to school every morning, feeling afraid. He wasn't afraid of school, or of his teacher, or of any of his lessons. He was afraid of two boys who went to the same school as he did.

Every morning these two boys lay in wait for Paul. He had to go down their lane, and sometimes they hid behind the big oak tree to jump out at him, and sometimes they hid behind the hedge. He never knew where they would be.

They never hurt him. They didn't kick or pinch or punch — they teased Paul in another way.

They threw his school cap over the hedge or up into a tree. They threw his school bag into the pond. They would take his lunch and scatter it over the grass. And Paul couldn't possibly stop them.

"You are cowards," he once said to John

and Alan. "You wouldn't do this to me if there was only one of you, because I could fight you then. But I can't fight two of you. I shall report you to our teacher if you do this any more."

"Well, if you tell tales, we'll tease you all the more," said Alan.

"We might even take off your shoes and stockings and put them on the old goat over there," said John.

Well, Paul knew quite well that they were likely to do what they said, for they didn't seem to care a bit what they did. So he didn't tell. He didn't like telling tales anyway, but he became very miserable about his teasing, because he got into trouble at home and at school over his lost caps, his wet school-bag and books, and his excuses over his lost lunch.

"Surely there must be times when it's best to tell tales?" he thought to himself. "Why should I keep getting into trouble like this for things that are not my fault? Still—I should get into worse trouble from John and Alan if they knew I'd told tales

—they might begin to pinch and kick me. I'm too small to fight both of them at once."

Well, things went on like this all through the summer term. Poor Paul had to have two new caps, because John threw one of his into the middle of a gorse bush far too prickly to rescue it from, and then Alan threw the second cap up a telegraph post and it hung there on the top of the post, impossible to reach.

Twice Paul was scolded and punished for bringing school books soaking wet to school. But how could he help it? John had again thrown his bag into the pond, scaring all the ducks, and soaking everything inside the bag.

And then one day something happened. Paul was going along to school, a little earlier than usual, hoping to slip down the lane before John and Alan came along. And up the lane came a funny little man, whose pointed ears showed that he was half a brownie.

It was Mr. Pink-Whistle, of course, but nobody could know it was because he couldn't be seen. He was invisible, but he had quite forgotten that, and was stamping along gaily, whistling loudly.

Now, half-way down the lane John and Alan were hiding behind a tree, waiting for Paul, and when they heard the footsteps and the whistling they felt sure it was Paul coming along as usual. So, to

Mr. Pink-Whistle's enormous astonishment, the two boys suddenly leapt out as he came by, shouting fiercely, their arms outstretched to catch Paul. But Paul wasn't there — no one was there! They couldn't see Pink-Whistle — and they couldn't hear him either, now, for he had stopped walking in amazement and was no longer whistling.

"Well!" said John, in astonishment. "I thought I heard Paul. But there's no one here!"

"I heard steps and whistling," said Alan. "Oh, look — there's Paul — coming down the lane. Come on, let's give his mack to the old goat to eat! Before Paul can get it away from him, he'll have munched big holes in it!"

Mr. Pink-Whistle listened to all this in the greatest surprise. Give a mackintosh to a goat to eat? These boys must be mad!

John and Alan pounced on poor Paul. They dragged his dark blue mack off his arm. "The old goat wants it for his dinner!" said Alan, with a grin.

"No, don't," said Paul, in alarm. "My mother has just paid a lot of money for that mack. It's new. Don't be so mean."

But the mack was wrenched away and thrown over the hedge for the goat to eat. Paul was left to try and get it back whilst the other boys ran off to school, laughing.

"Beasts!" said Paul, climbing over the hedge to get his mack. The goat had already bitten off a button. "Why don't they leave me alone? They throw my caps away, they throw my bag into the pond, they spoil everything of mine that they can. And I can't stop them! Nobody can!"

"Excuse me — but I think I can do something about it," said Mr. Pink-Whistle, appearing so suddenly that both Paul and the goat jumped in surprise. The goat dropped the mack and ran away. Paul stood and stared at Pink-Whistle in amazement.

"Where did you come from?" he asked. "You suddenly appeared!"

"Yes. I forgot I was invisible," said Pink-

Whistle. "I didn't mean to give you quite such a shock. Let me have a look at that mack."

There was a big tear in it and a button was gone. It was in the goat, so there was no getting that back. But somehow Pink-Whistle managed to mend the mack. A new button seemed to grow in the right place, and the big tear pressed its edges together, gave a peculiar kind of squeak and disappeared.

"I say," said Paul, half-scared. "I say —you're a bit magic, aren't you?"

"Just a bit," said Pink-Whistle. "Now —you'd better rush off to school, or you'll be late. Leave things to me. I have a feeling I'm going to interfere a little. If you want to see a bit of fun, hide behind that tree at the end of the morning."

Paul stared hard at Pink-Whistle. He couldn't make him out. He liked the little man very much indeed, and he thought he had the brightest twinkle in his eyes that he had ever seen. He nodded, put his mack over his arm, and sped off to school, wondering what was going to happen.

At the end of the morning Paul shot off before John and Alan left. Now it was his turn to hide behind the tree — not to pounce out, but to watch. He couldn't see Mr. Pink-Whistle anywhere. He wondered if he could have imagined him.

But Pink-Whistle was there all right. He had made himself invisible again, that was all. He waited for John and Alan, and very soon along they came, kicking a stone between them.

"Excuse me," said Pink-Whistle, in a loud but polite voice. The boys stopped in surprise. They could see no one.

"I want to borrow your caps," said Pink-Whistle, still very polite. To the two boys' dismay their caps suddenly whisked off their heads, flew up into the air and landed on the exact tops of two chimneys belonging to a near-by cottage.

"And now your shoes, please," said Pink-Whistle, and their laces were undone, and their shoes pulled off, before they knew what was happening!

Up into the air went the four shoes. Two landed on the old billy-goat's horns and two on the horns of a most astonished cow. Neither of the boys dared go and get them. The cow looked angry and the goat knew how to butt very hard.

"Fine," said Pink-Whistle, who still couldn't be seen. "So kind of you to let me have your things. But still, why not? You take Paul's things, don't you? So, of course, you are willing to lend me yours."

"Who's speaking? Who's doing all this?" said John, clutching Alan's arm.

Behind the tree there sounded a chuckle. It came from Paul, who was really enjoying himself. Now Alan and John knew what it was like to be teased and not be able to stop the teaser!

Mr. Pink-Whistle hadn't nearly finished. No, when he did a thing he did it really thoroughly!

He stripped off the boys' stockings next, made the billy-goat stand still, and then slipped them on to each leg. The goat was rather pleased. The stockings were warm, he felt grand in them, and he could always eat them when he was tired of them. He trotted round the field in them, looking rather peculiar because he still had a pair of shoes on his horns.

Alan and John were very scared by now, and began to run away. But a strong and firm hand took hold of each of them.

"No, don't go. I would like to borrow your school-bags, please."

So off came their school satchels. One sailed away to the top of a tall chestnut tree, and the other fell into the stream and sailed down it merrily, with pens, pencils, and papers leaking out of it. Oh dear, now they couldn't do their homework, and the teacher would be very angry!

Their ties came off next, flew up towards the telegraph wires and then tied themselves round a wire in neat bows. It was really most extraordinary. Even Paul forgot to laugh for a moment, and felt a bit scared. This little invisible man must know a lot of magic!

"Don't!" begged Alan, in alarm, holding on to his coat and shorts, afraid that they would go next. "Don't! Who are you, doing this? Don't do any more!"

Mr. Pink-Whistle hadn't quite finished. He pulled out the boys' handkerchiefs, threw them into the field, and the goat at once ate them both. He didn't really mind what he ate. He had once tried to eat a tin and many times he had eaten newspapers, rope, paper-bags, and cardboard cartons. So he was quite pleased with the handkerchiefs.

"Well, thank you very much," said Mr. Pink-Whistle politely. "That's all for this morning. I'll meet you here again another day perhaps. That would be very nice."

"No, oh no!" cried Alan and John, and fled down the lane in their bare feet as fast as they could go. Paul came out from behind the tree, laughing.

"I don't know quite where you are," he said to Mr. Pink-Whistle, who was still invisible, "but thank you very much for interfering. Oh dear, look at those caps on the chimneys still."

Pink-Whistle suddenly appeared, looking very pleased with himself. "Yes, they look comic up there, don't they?" he said. "I did enjoy myself. Well, my boy, I have a feeling that those two boys won't tease you much more. I don't believe they liked my bit of interference! I'll be along here again for the next few days, so call out if you want me."

But Paul didn't call out, because John and Alan never went down that lane again. They were so afraid of meeting the polite and powerful little invisible man that they went another way to school. It took them twice as long, so they had to start much earlier. Paul never had any bother with them again.

The funny thing is the school ties are still tied in bows round the telegraph wire. Nobody can imagine who put them there — but if you see them you'll know. It was all because Mr. Pink-Whistle interfered!

VII

MR. PINK-WHISTLE IS RATHER FUNNY

Once when Mr. Pink-Whistle was walking down a rather lonely road he met a small boy who was crying bitterly.

Pink-Whistle could never bear to see anyone unhappy, and stopped at once.

"What's the matter?" he said. "You tell me what's the matter, and maybe I can put it right."

"My mother s-s-sent me to buy some b-b-bread," wept the small boy, "and the boy who lives round the corner took the money from me and ran off with it. And my mother will s-s-s-spank me."

"Dear, dear!" said Pink-Whistle. "I'm very sorry to hear that. Come with me, and we'll buy the bread together. Then maybe if we meet this bad boy you can point him out to me."

So they went to the baker's shop together and bought some bread.

Pink-Whistle paid for it, and they went out in the street again.

But the bad boy was nowhere to be seen. So Pink-Whistle said good-bye and sent the small boy home.

He set off down the road again, a little plump man with the pointed ears of a brownie, and a merry, twinkling look in his eyes. But soon he heard the sound of sobbing again, and he saw two little girls running on the opposite side of the road, tears pouring down their red cheeks.

"Dear, dear me!" said Pink-Whistle to himself. "All the children seem to be in tears to-day!"

He ran across and stopped the two little girls. They hadn't any hankies, so he dried their tears with his great big one.

"Now, you tell me what's wrong," he said.

"Well, we were going to the sweet-shop to buy some chocolate," said one of the little girls, "and a horrid boy came up to us and asked us where we were going.

106

And when we told him we were going to the sweet shop he said how much money had we?"

"And when we showed him, he snatched it out of our hands and ran away," wept the other little girl. "So we can't buy our chocolate, and we saved up a whole week for it."

"Well, well," said Pink-Whistle, holding out his hand. "Come along and we'll go and buy some. I don't think that bad boy will stop you if you are with *me*."

So they all went to the sweet-shop, and Pink-Whistle bought plenty of chocolate for the two little girls. They beamed at him.

"Oh, thank you! You *are* kind!" they said. "We do hope we shan't meet that big boy and have him take our chocolate from us!"

"I'll see you right home," said Pink-Whistle. So off they went, and he saw them safely home. But they didn't meet the bad boy as Pink-Whistle had hoped they would.

Now, just after he had left them, what should he hear but yet another child crying. Surely it couldn't be someone that bad boy had robbed again? Mr. Pink-Whistle hurried round the corner to see.

A very small girl was there, holding the corner of her dress to her eyes. "He took the sausages!" she wept. "He dragged them away from me!"

"Who did?" asked Pink-Whistle sharply.

"A bad boy," wept the tiny girl. "My mother will smack me for coming home without the sausages. It's that bad boy. He takes everything we have."

Well, Pink-Whistle had to buy a string of sausages then. It was really quite an expensive morning for him. He didn't see the bad boy. He wondered where he was.

"Nobody really knows," said the little girl, who was now all smiles again, trotting along by Pink-Whistle, holding tightly to his hand. "You see, he hides — and pounces out. We never see him come. He runs so fast, too, no one can ever catch him."

"I see," said Pink-Whistle. "Well, I shall look out for him!"

"You'll never see him," said the tiny girl. "He only pounces out on children smaller than himself. If you were a child, going shopping, you would see him soon enough!"

Pink-Whistle thought that was a good idea. Of course — he was sure to see that bad boy if he were a small child! It was only small children he robbed.

So, as soon as the small girl had run in at her gate, Pink-Whistle stepped into a lonely passage and muttered a few magic words. And no sooner were the words said than he had gone as small as a child of six!

He looked a bit queer because he still wore his own clothes. But that didn't bother Pink-Whistle.

He murmured a few more words and hey presto, he was dressed like a little boy, in jersey and grey shorts!

Pink-Whistle set out along the street, carrying a big teddy-bear, which had appeared at the same time as the jersey and shorts. He met one or two grown-ups who didn't take any notice of him at all.

He turned down another road where there was not a soul to be seen. He had gone about half-way when he came to an empty house and garden — and out of the gate darted a big boy, about fourteen, with a horrid, spiteful face.

"Stop," said the big boy, and Pink-

Whistle stopped. "Give me that bear!" said the boy.

"No," said Pink-Whistle. But the boy snatched the bear roughly from his hands and ran off with it.

He didn't run far, because something very queer happened. The bear bit him!

The bad boy felt the nip in his hand and looked down in astonishment. He thought something had stung him. The bear bit him again, and the boy cried out in alarm. He tried to drop the teddy bear, but the bear hung on to him for all it was worth, biting and nipping whenever it could find a bit of flesh.

"Oooh!" said the boy in great alarm. "Are you alive? Stop it! That hurt!"

But the bear climbed all over him, biting and snapping, having a perfectly lovely time. Then it slipped down the boy's leg and ran all the way back to Pink-Whistle. The little man whispered to it and it disappeared into thin air. So did Pink-Whistle.

He followed the bad boy, then slipped ahead of him, made himself visible and turned back to meet him again. There was no one else about at all.

As Pink-Whistle, who had now changed himself into a little girl, came near the bad boy, he jingled some money in his hand. The bad boy stopped at once.

"Give me that money!"

"No," said Pink-Whistle, and pretended to cry in fright, like a little girl. The bad boy caught hold of his hand, forced it open roughly and took out the pennies Pink-Whistle was holding. He ran off with them.

Pink-Whistle stood and watched. Presently the bad boy stopped and looked down at the money in his hand. The pennies seemed to be awfully hot!

"Funny!" said the boy. "They are almost burning my hand, they're so hot! Ow! I'll put them into my pockets!"

So he did — but they got hotter and hotter and hotter, and the boy could feel them burning a hole and hurting him! Then, to his horror, he saw smoke coming from his pockets! He turned them inside out and the pennies rolled away. But oh, what holes they had burnt!

The bad boy went on, puzzled. He didn't hear Pink-Whistle coming past him, invisible, his feet making no noise at all.

And when he met the little man again, he did not look like Mr. Pink-Whistle, but like a sturdy little boy, carrying a small bag in which were some fine glass marbles.

The bad boy stopped and looked at the bag. "What's in there?" he said roughly.

"My marbles," said Pink-Whistle, in a little-boy voice.

"Let me see them," said the bad boy.

"No," said Pink-Whistle.

"You let me see them!" roared the bad boy, and Pink-Whistle meekly opened the bag. In a trice the big boy snatched it away, marbles and all, for he could see what fine ones they were.

Then off he ran. Pink-Whistle stood and watched him.

The bag felt very heavy after a bit. The boy looked down at it. It seemed bigger than he thought — almost a little sack. He decided to put it over his shoulder. It would be easier to carry that way.

So he put it over his left shoulder and set off again. But with every step he took the sack felt heavier and heavier and heavier. It weighed the boy down. He tried to take it off his shoulder, but he couldn't. He panted and puffed, and at last stopped, almost squashed to bits under the enormous weight.

Some children came running by and they stopped in surprise to see the bad boy weighed down by the enormous sack. They all knew him. He had taken things from each one of them at some time or other.

"What a horrid smell the sack has!" said one child. "What's in it?"

"Help me to get it off my shoulder!" begged the bad boy. One of the children slit a hole in the sack — and out came a stream of rotten apples!

"Ho! He's carrying rotten apples!" cried the child. "Where did you steal those?"

"They're marbles, not apples!" said the bad boy, in surprise. But they weren't. He was carrying nothing but hundreds of rotten apples! How extraordinary!

And then the children had a lovely time. They pulled the sack away from the bad boy, spilt all the rotten apples, and pelted him with them as hard as they could. Pink-Whistle joined in, you may be sure. A good punishment was just what the bad boy needed!

He ran off at last, crying bitterly, for he was not at all brave. Pink-Whistle, now looking like a little girl, met him as he went down the road. Pink-Whistle carried a hand-bag, and felt certain that the boy would stop.

But he didn't. He had had enough of taking things away from children. There was something queer about that day. So

Pink-Whistle, looking just like a nice little girl, stopped the boy instead.

"I've got a whole shilling in my bag!" said Pink-Whistle, shaking it so that the money jingled.

"Keep it!" said the bad boy, wiping his dirty, tear-stained face.

"There's nobody about. You can easily take it away from me!" said Pink-Whistle.

"I'm never going to take anything from anyone again," said the boy. "Never!"

Pink-Whistle suddenly changed into himself again, and to the boy's enormous surprise the little girl was no longer there — but a solemn-faced little man stood in front of him.

"Do you mean that?" asked Pink-Whistle, sternly. "Or do you want a few more lessons?"

"Oh, no, no!" cried the boy. "I'd be afraid of stopping anyone now. You've no idea the awful things that have happened to me to-day!"

"Serves you right," said Pink-Whistle. "Now you listen to me. You be kind in future to all those children you've stolen from, and give them pennies and sweets whenever you can. That will show me you're sorry. See? Else maybe awful things will happen to you again!"

"I will, I will," promised the bad boy, and ran home, frightened and worried. He thought about it the whole afternoon, and decided that he had better keep his word.

So, to the great astonishment of all the small children round about, the bad boy stopped them and gave them things, instead of taking things away from them. And soon they were very fond of him, and ran to meet him whenever they saw him.

"I wish I could meet that funny little fellow again and tell him how much happier I am now," the bad boy thought to himself a great many times. "He might like me. I wish I could meet him."

But Pink-Whistle was far away by that time, putting something else right. I do hope he comes along if anything goes wrong for you!

VIII

MR. PINK-WHISTLE AND THE MONEY-BOX

For some time Mr. Pink-Whistle hadn't come across anything to put right, and he was feeling very pleased about it.

"Perhaps the world is getting a better place," he thought to himself. "Perhaps people are being nicer to one another, and kinder. Maybe I needn't go around any more looking for things to put right. Perhaps I can go back to my own little cottage and live there peacefully with Sooty, my cat."

But that very day Pink-Whistle had to change his mind, because he found two very unhappy children.

Pink-Whistle was walking in the lane that ran at the back of their garden, and he heard one of the children crying.

"Never mind," said a boy's voice. "Never mind, Katie. We shall have to save up again, that's all."

"But it was such a mean thing to do to us," sobbed Katie. "That's what's making me cry. It was such a horrid, mean, unkind thing."

Pink-Whistle peeped over the wall. He saw two children nearby — a boy and a girl. They both looked very upset, but the boy wasn't crying.

"What's the matter?" asked Pink-Whistle. "Can I do anything to help?"

"No, I'm afraid not," said the boy. "You see, it's like this. Katie and I have been saving up for our mother's birthday — we know exactly what she wants — that big red shawl in the draper's. It's a lovely one."

"I know. I've seen it," said Pink-Whistle.

"Well, it costs a lot of money," said the boy. "But Katie and I have been doing all kinds of jobs to earn the money for it."

"We ran errands and we delivered papers," said Katie, rubbing her eyes.

"I helped the farmer to lift his potatoes," said the boy. "And that's hard work."

"And I took Mrs. Brown's baby out each day for a week when she was ill," said Katie. "She gave me sixpence for that."

"And I weeded old Mr. Kent's garden, and he gave me a shilling," said the boy. "We put it all into our money-box pig."

"Oh, was your money-box in the shape

of a pig?" asked Mr. Pink-Whistle. "I like that sort of money-box."

"It was a tin pig, painted pink, and it had a slit in its back," said Katie. "And it had a little key hanging on its tail to unlock a sort of little door in its tummy. We got the money out of the little door when we wanted it."

"The pig was so nice and full," said the boy. "It jingled when we shook it. We were sure we had nearly enough to buy the shawl, and it is Mother's birthday next week. But now all our money is gone!"

"Where's it gone?" said Pink-Whistle, surprised.

"Someone stole it," said Katie, her eyes filling with tears again. "We took it out here in the garden, meaning to count out the money. Then Mother called us in for our biscuits and we ran indoors, and when we came out the pig was gone, and all the money with it."

"Somebody must have come by, looked over the wall, and seen the money-box pig," said the boy, sadly. "Now all our hard work is wasted — and we shall never get enough money to buy that shawl."

"It really is a shame," said Mr. Pink-Whistle, getting quite red with anger. "It's not fair that someone should come along and take all the money you've worked hard to get. Perhaps I have got some for you. Wait a minute. Let me look in my pockets."

But Pink-Whistle had only two pennies that day, so that wasn't much use. He rubbed one of his pointed ears and frowned. What could he do? He must do something!

Someone called the children. "We must go," said Katie. "It's time for our dinner. Thank you for being so nice."

The children ran off. Mr. Pink-Whistle went on down the lane, remembering the girl's tear-stained face and the boy's look of disappointment. What a shame to steal from children!

"Well, I shall do something!" said Pink-Whistle, fiercely. "But I don't know what. It seems to me as if all I can do is to poke my nose into every house I see, and try to find that money-box pig!"

So he made himself invisible, and began to peep into the windows of all the houses he passed. But he didn't see any money-box pig at all.

He went on and on, peering into kitchens and sitting-rooms, trying to discover a money-box pig — and at last he found one!

It was standing on the mantelpiece of a neat little cottage, next to a ticking clock. There was a man in the room, reading. He looked smart and clean and neat — but Pink-Whistle didn't really like his face.

"Too clever!" thought Pink-Whistle. "Too sharp! He looks as if he would do people a bad turn if he could, and think himself clever to do it! And there's the money-box pig, standing on the mantelpiece. Can it be the pig the children had stolen from them? Surely this well-dressed man here wouldn't steal such a thing as a child's money-box. He looks quite well-off."

Someone went up the path and knocked at the door. The man inside looked up, got up quickly, took the money-box pig and put it under a cushion. Then Pink-Whistle knew he had stolen it. "Aha!" said the little man to himself, "aha! He wouldn't hide it if he hadn't stolen it. The mean fellow!"

The man opened the door to his friend, and Pink-Whistle slipped in beside him. He was quite invisible, so no one knew he was there.

"You're early," said the first man. "The others haven't arrived yet."

"Oho!" thought Pink-Whistle, "so there is to be a meeting. I think I'll stay—and have a bit of fun!"

So he stood in a corner, and then, when he had a chance to do it, he slipped his hand under the cushion and took out the pig. He stood it on the mantelpiece.

He shook it and the money jingled. Then Pink-Whistle made a grunting noise, just like a little pig, and spoke in a funny, piggy voice.

"Take me back, take me back!"

Mr. Crooky, the man who lived in the cottage, looked up, very startled, and so did his friend. It seemed to them as if the money-box pig on the mantelpiece was jigging up and down and talking. They couldn't see Pink-Whistle moving it, of course.

"How extraordinary!" said the friend. Mr. Crooky got up and took hold of the pig very roughly. He took it into the kitchen and put it on the dresser there. He slammed the door and came back. There was a knock at the front door and two more men came into the meeting.

Pink-Whistle grinned. He slipped quietly into the kitchen, found the pig, came back, shut the kitchen door softly, and, when no one was looking, placed the pig on the mantelpiece again!

Then he jiggled it hard and grunted in a piggy way again, talking in a funny, squeaky voice. "Take me back! Take me back! I don't belong to you. Take me back!"

All the four men stopped talking and stared in astonishment at the jigging pig. Mr. Crooky went very red and looked most alarmed. How had that pig got down from the dresser, opened the kitchen door, and got back to the mantelpiece? How was it that it grunted and jigged and talked like that? It must be magic!

"'What does it mean, saying that it wants to be taken back?" asked one of the men. "Doesn't it belong to you?"

"Of course it does," said Mr. Crooky. "I can't imagine what's come over the pig. I never knew a tin pig behave like that before."

"Oh, you bad story-teller, oh, you wicked man!" squeaked Pink-Whistle, making the pig dance all round the mantelpiece as if it was angry. "You stole me! You know you did! Take me back, take me back!"

"This is very strange," said one of the men looking hard at Crooky. "What does it mean?"

"Nothing. It's just a silly joke of some sort," said Mr. Crooky, beginning to tremble. "I'll throw the pig into the dust-bin."

So he snatched it up, went into the yard and threw the pig hard into the dust-bin. He slammed on the lid and went back to the house. How tiresome of this to happen just when he had called a meeting to ask his friends to give him money to start a shop! Now they might not trust him!

Pink-Whistle had gone into the yard with Mr. Crooky. As soon as Crooky had gone back, Pink-Whistle took off the lid and fished out the pig. It was covered with tea-leaves.

Pink-Whistle crept to the window. It was open. To the men's enormous surprise, the money-box pig suddenly appeared on the window-sill, jigging and capering like mad, and a grunting voice could be heard at the same time. Then came the squeaky, piggy voice.

"You bad man! You put me in the dust-bin! I'm covered with tea-leaves — but you ought to be covered with shame! You stole me from those children. You know you did. Take me back, take me back!"

"This is most extraordinary and most disgraceful," said one of the men, standing up. "Mr. Crooky, take that pig back at once. If you don't, I shall call the village policeman and ask him to listen to all the pig says."

Mr. Crooky felt as if he were in a bad dream. He stared at the pig, which turned a somersault and rattled like mad. "I'm hungry!" it squeaked, "I'm hungry. You put something into me, quick! I'm hungree-eeeeeeeeh!"

Mr. Crooky felt so frightened that he put his hand into his pocket and pulled out all the money there. He popped it into the slit in the pig's back.

"More, more!" cried the pig, and Mr. Crooky put in more and more till he had no money left. "Now take me home, home, home!" cried the pig, and leapt high into the air and back again to the window-sill. Mr. Crooky thought that either he or the pig must be mad, or perhaps both of them. Or maybe it was a frightening kind of dream.

"Well, I'd better take you back, and then perhaps I shall wake up," he said. So he snatched up the dancing pig, and ran off with it at top speed. He came to the children's garden and threw the pig over the wall. It landed on the grass.

Mr. Crooky turned to go home. "Now don't you *ever* do such a wicked thing again!" a voice boomed in his ear, making him almost jump out of his skin. It was Mr. Pink-Whistle, of course, having one last smack at Mr. Crooky. The man tore off down the lane as if a hundred dogs were after him. Mr. Pink-Whistle made himself visible and climbed over the wall into the garden. He called the children.

They came running to him and he showed them the pig, which he had picked up. "Here you are," he said. "Safely back again—and heavier than before."

The children shouted with delight. They undid the little door in the pig's tummy and the money tumbled out. What a lot there was now!

"More than we ever put in!" cried Katie. "Oh, how marvellous! How did it happen, little man? Tell us, do!"

But Pink-Whistle had vanished again. He didn't like being thanked. It was enough to see the children's joyful faces, and to know that they could buy their mother the present they had saved up for — and could buy her something else besides now!

As for Mr. Crooky, he didn't get the money lent to him for the shop he wanted to start — and a very good thing, too! He is still puzzled whenever he thinks of that grunting, dancing, talking pig, but if he happens to read this story, he won't be puzzled any more!

IX

MR. PINK-WHISTLE HAS A GOOD IDEA

One day Mr. Pink-Whistle was going along down a quiet road, when he saw a face looking at him out of a window.

It was a nice face. It belonged to an old lady, whose hair shone silvery-grey in the sunshine, and whose eyes were blue and kind. But it was a sad face.

"I'll go by here to-morrow, and see if the old lady is still looking out," thought Pink-Whistle. "I shall be seeing that poor old pony in the field at the bottom of this road every day for some time, so I can easily come down this road and look out for the old lady."

Mr. Pink-Whistle had made a new friend —a very old pony, who had worked hard all his life long, pulling heavy carts, and taking his master to market.

He would have been very happy if he had had a kind master, but the man he worked for was rough and impatient, too ready with the whip, and always shouting.

And now, when the pony was too old to pull heavy carts any more, and had been shut into the field, he was lonely and afraid.

"You see," he said to Pink-Whistle, who, being half a brownie, understood animals very well, "you see, Mr. Pink-Whistle, I'm afraid that my master, now that I am no good to him, may sell me off to someone who will work me to death, and I really feel very tired and old now. I could do a little light work, but I'm afraid I couldn't do heavy work any more. I should fall down, and then I should be lashed and shouted at."

"It's a shame," said Pink-Whistle. "It really is. But perhaps your master won't sell you to anyone who will work you like that. He certainly is not a kind or just man, but I don't believe his wife would let him do anything horrid to you."

"He might even sell me to be killed and sold as horse-flesh," said the poor old pony. "You see, I really am no use to him

134

now! I might pull a baby's pram, but I couldn't pull a cart any more. Oh, Mr. Pink-Whistle, I do feel so lonely and afraid sometimes. I don't know what I should do if you didn't come and talk to me."

"Now I really can't bear this," thought kind Pink-Whistle to himself, each time he left the old pony. "What am I to do? I must put this right somehow, but how?

Nobody wants a pony like that, and yet he deserves a little kindness and friendliness now, after having worked so hard and well all his life. It isn't fair."

It wasn't fair. The farmer should have gone sometimes to the field, patted the old pony, and cheered him up. He should have told him that he could live out the rest of his days in peace and sunshine. But he didn't. He just grumbled because he couldn't get any more work out of him.

"If I could hear of anyone that wants an old pony like that I'd sell him," he said to his wife. "He's perfectly useless to me, but anyone with an old cab could still get a bit of work out of him."

"Well, it's a good thing that there are so few horse-cabs now," said his wife. "I'd hate you to sell old Brownie to a cabman, who might whip him and try to make his poor old legs go faster than they can."

Pink-Whistle thought a lot about the old pony. Anyone or anything in trouble made his kind heart very heavy and sad. And now he began to worry about the old lady who looked out of the window he passed every day.

"She looks so sad and lonely. She's got the same look in her eyes as the old pony. When people get old and tired they shouldn't be allowed to be sad and lonely."

Every day he looked at the old lady and soon he began to smile and wave as he passed. She smiled back and waved, too. Each time Pink-Whistle went to see the old pony he kept a special smile for the old lady in the window.

Then one day he found some marigolds growing wild on a rubbish-heap at the bottom of the field where the old pony lived. "I'll take those to the old lady!" thought Pink-Whistle. So he picked them, made them into a nice little bunch, and that day, instead of passing the gate where the old lady lived, he opened it and marched up to the door!

But nobody opened it. A voice from the window said: "I'm so sorry I can't open the door. I can't walk without help. Will you come to the window?"

So Pink-Whistle went to the window, beamed at the old lady, and gave her the marigolds. She put them into a glass of water and beamed back.

"How kind you are!" she said. "I always look for your smile as you go down the street. Where do you go?"

Pink-Whistle told her about the old pony. The old woman listened with great interest.

"Poor old thing," she said. "Once I used to be rich and I had a pony-cart and pony of my own, and I used to drive about. Now I am poor, and somehow I have no friends. I am a poor, helpless old woman, no use to anyone—just like the old pony!"

"Can't you walk?" asked Pink-Whistle. "If you could get about a bit you could soon make friends!"

"No, I can't walk," said the old lady. "There is something wrong with my legs. I did have a good friend who came in every day to take me out in my bath-chair —but now she has moved far away, and the woman who said she would come is cross and busy—too busy to take me out at all. She cleans my room for me, and helps me in and out of bed—but she can't spare the time to take me out."

"So you never go out?" said Pink-Whistle. "Well, well—what a pity! You must be very lonely and dull. I must come and see you sometimes."

So he went to see her, and one day he pulled out the bath-chair from the cupboard it had stood in for months and managed to get the old lady tucked up in it. Then out they went — and the first thing Pink-Whistle did was to take her to see the old pony!

Well, you can guess how the two old things liked one another! The old lady had always loved horses — and the pony was delighted to find someone who knew how to talk to him, and click to him, and offer him a carrot. He nuzzled his brown head into her shoulder, and it was all Pink-Whistle could do to make them part.

One day the old lady was very excited. She had had a letter from her friend — and in it was some money!

"Look!" she said to Pink-Whistle. "Money! But I don't want money at my age. So I am going to give it all to you, dear Mr. Pink-Whistle, every bit — and you must buy a present for yourself from a grateful old lady. I don't know what I should have done without you."

"I don't want your money," said Pink-Whistle, smiling. "You keep it and buy

yourself a new shawl and a new armchair."

The old lady's eyes filled with tears. "I don't want anything for myself," she said. "I did so want you to have the money, Mr. Pink-Whistle. There is nothing I can do for you, nothing at all, in return for the happiness you have given to me—and I did think, I really did think this would be a little return for all your kindness."

Pink-Whistle didn't know what to do. He felt as if he couldn't take money from the old lady—and yet she would be terribly unhappy if he didn't. After all, it *is* lovely to pay back kindness—and there was no other way she could do it.

And then a grand idea came into Pink-Whistle's head, and he grinned his wide grin. He held out his hand. "I'll take the money," he said, "but on one condition, old friend—that I can do exactly as I like with it!"

"Of course you can," said the old lady gladly, and gave him the money. Pink-Whistle trotted off quickly, full of his idea.

He went to the farmer who lived in his farmhouse beside the pony's field. He asked him how much the old pony was.

There was enough money to buy him. "May I keep him in the field when he is not in use?" asked Pink-Whistle. The farmer said yes. Pink-Whistle trotted back to the old lady's house. He pulled out her bath-chair, and went off with it. She didn't see him, because she was asleep.

The little man took the chair to a leather-worker and asked him to fit it up so that it could be drawn along by a pony. "That's easy," said the man. "You'll want reins, of course — and little shafts put here — and this bit altered there. I can do it in two days."

"I'll help you, Dad," said the man's small boy, a smiling, merry-eyed lad. "'Tisn't often we do a job like this, is it? I'd like to see a pony drawing this bath-chair. Is there a pony for it, Mister?"

"Yes," said Pink-Whistle, and told the boy all about it. Then a good idea came to him. "I suppose you wouldn't like to fetch the pony from the field every day to the old lady's house, and harness him to the bath-chair for her, would you?" he said. "You're not very big and you could ride on the pony's back to and from the field."

"Oooooh, yes," said the small boy, his eyes shining with delight. "I love horses. I'd just love that. Dad, may I do that?"

Pink-Whistle left the workshop, feeling very pleased. He had spent the old lady's money well! He had done something that would make the old pony very happy, for now he would have a friend, a nice light job of work — and a little boy to talk to him and even ride on his back a little each day. And the small boy would have some fun and feel quite important riding the pony, and harnessing him to the bath-chair each day.

"Well, it's wonderful what can be done if you really think hard enough," said Pink-Whistle, trotting down the road very happily. "I do wonder what the old lady will say!"

Well, you should have seen her face the

first day that the little boy came into the garden riding the old pony! Pink-Whistle arrived too, with the altered bath-chair. The little boy jumped down, and fitted straps and reins as his father had shown him. They both smiled and waved at the astonished old lady.

Then Pink-Whistle went into the house

and helped the old lady to hobble slowly along to the bath-chair. She couldn't walk properly, she could only hobble a few steps. She got into the chair and Pink-Whistle tucked her up. He gave her the reins.

"Now, you said you know how to drive a horse," he said. "You needn't be afraid that the pony will go fast, because he won't. He's too old. He's so pleased to come and do a job of work like this for you. He's yours. I bought him with your money. Now — off you go!"

And off they went, the old lady driving the pony, and steering the bath-chair at the same time in a very clever way — but as the pony only walked slowly, there wasn't any danger of the old lady having an accident at all.

"Well, that's a fine sight to see, isn't it?" said Pink-Whistle, pleased, as he stared down the road after the two old friends, his hand on the small boy's shoulder. "Now, you look out for them to come back — and take out the pony and ride him back to the field. Look after the old

lady, too, and help her into the house."

Good old Pink-Whistle! The old lady is as happy as she can be, driving out with her pony every day—and the old pony isn't afraid or lonely any more, because she is his friend. And he has the little boy, too, to talk to him and ride him carefully, and bring him a lump of sugar for a treat.

But the happiest of them all is Pink-Whistle, of course. "There's nothing like putting bad things right," he says. "It's the finest thing anyone can do."

I think so, too, don't you?

X

MR. PINK-WHISTLE AND THE EGGS

Annabelle had five hens. Granpa had given them to her on her last birthday, when they were quite small. Now they were big, and just beginning to lay.

Annabelle was delighted. "Mummy, you shall have an egg for your breakfast every day!" she said. "And so shall Daddy. And I will take two round to Granny and Granpa every day, and there will be one egg for my breakfast, too. You will lay me five eggs, won't you, little red hens?"

The five hens looked at Annabelle and clucked. They liked this little girl who fed them each day, gave them fresh water, and cleaned out their house three times a week. They liked the way she talked to them, too. So they all clucked back, and Annabelle knew quite well what they said.

"They say they will certainly lay me five eggs every day," she told her mother.

They did. Each morning when little

Annabelle went to look in the nesting-boxes there were five smooth brown eggs. Not very big ones, because the hens were young, but, oh, how delicious they tasted!

Daddy and Mummy had one each day. So did Annabelle. She took two round to Granny and Granpa, always the biggest two, because it was Granpa who had given her the little red hens.

And then one morning when Annabelle went to look for the eggs there was not a single one! All the nesting-boxes were empty. What a shock for Annabelle. She stared at the empty boxes and then at the hens.

"Why haven't you laid me any eggs?" she said.

The hens clucked loudly. "Cuck-cuck-cuck, we did, we did!" they said.

"You didn't," said Anabelle. "There aren't any at all. Please lay me some to-morrow."

But there weren't any the next day either. Annabelle couldn't understand it. "Perhaps someone is taking them," she thought. "Oh, dear, what a horrid thing to do."

The next day there were no eggs again. Annabelle cried bitterly. "It's a shame!" she said to the hens. "I am sure somebody is stealing your eggs. It's a shame! You are my own hens, and you lay beautiful eggs that are mine—and now somebody else is taking them."

A big black cat with green eyes was

151

wandering by, not far from the hen-house. It stopped when it heard Annabelle crying, and listened to what she said.

Then it ran off quickly to its master. The cat was Sooty, Mr. Pink-Whistle's own cat. It mewed for its master, and Mr. Pink-Whistle came hurrying from the kitchen, where he was busy cleaning out his larder.

"A job for you to do, Master!" mewed Sooty. "You leave the larder to me. I'll clean it all right! I've found a better job for you to do than that."

"What is it?" asked Mr. Pink-Whistle. "Is it something I can put right? I haven't done a job like that for some time."

"Yes, you can put it right, I expect," said Sooty, and told Mr. Pink-Whistle what had happened to Annabelle. "She's such a dear little girl," said Sooty. "And somebody is really being very unkind, Master, to steal all her eggs."

"I'll soon put that right!" said Mr. Pink-Whistle, briskly. "Where does she live? Oh, not very far away. That's good."

Now, the next morning, just as it was beginning to get light, Mr. Pink-Whistle went out. He made his way to Annabelle's house. Just as he turned in at her front gate he made himself invisible. Hey, presto! One moment he was there, and the next he was not. At least, he was, but nobody could see him.

He went down the garden to the hen-house. Scamp, the dog, heard him and smelt him, but couldn't see him. He growled a little in fright but didn't bark.

Mr. Pink-Whistle went right to the bottom of the garden, where a tall hedge stood. Just beside it was the hen-house. Mr. Pink-Whistle had a look round. Nobody about just yet. He opened the henhouse door and felt in the nesting-boxes. Four eggs already—and a hen sitting in the fifth box!

He went out and shut the door softly. Then he stood on the path and waited in the dim light. He felt certain that the thief would soon be coming along, whoever he was.

Then very softly and silently, so that even Scamp's sharp ears heard no sound, somebody came through a gap in the hedge. Pink-Whistle looked at him. Dear, dear—who ever would have thought him to be the thief?

"It's Mr. Smarmy," said Pink-Whistle to himself. "He goes to church. He sings hymns very loudly indeed. He always shakes his head and looks shocked when he hears of someone who has done wrong. And all the time he is taking little Annabelle's eggs!"

Mr. Smarmy was well-dressed and neat. Even coming through the hedge had not made him untidy. He tiptoed to the hen-house, opened the door, and felt about for eggs. One, two, three, four, five. Good! He put them carefully into his five pockets, and then went out. He backed through the hedge and pulled the branches together behind him. He was gone.

"So it's Mr. Smarmy," said Pink-Whistle again. "I never did like him. Always so down on other people. Always finding fault with his gentle little wife. Always pretending to be so good and proper. Dear, dear—what a very horrid fellow, to be sure. I never did like deceitful people. Now what's to be done?"

Pink-Whistle went off to his own home. He went to his larder and looked in the egg-rack. There were six eggs there. He took five of them. He went back to the hen-house and popped them into the nesting boxes. "Now Annabelle won't be disappointed!" he said. "And to-morrow I'll play a nice little trick on Mr. Smarmy."

The eggs were white ones, not brown. Annabelle was most astonished when she found them that morning. "Look, Mummy!" she said. "There are eggs this morning all right—but they are white, not brown. Isn't that queer?"

Now, that day Mr. Pink-Whistle spent in a very queer way. He made five magic eggs, and how he chuckled as he made them. Sooty watched him and chuckled too.

Early the next morning Mr. Pink-Whistle went along to Annabelle's hen-house again. There were five brown eggs there. He put them carefully into his pocket, and then put five magic eggs into the nesting-boxes instead. Then, quite invisible, he waited for Mr. Smarmy to come along. The thief came silently through the hedge. He went into the hen-house and put the eggs carefully into his five pockets. Then he went out again.

Mr. Pink-Whistle chuckled once more.

He waited till Mr. Smarmy had gone, then he popped back into the hen-house and put the brown eggs from his pocket into the nesting-boxes. Annabelle would find them there, quite safely.

Then he went home to breakfast. Sooty had got it ready for him. The big black cat laughed when he heard what his master had done.

"One of the magic eggs will go POP very loudly indeed," said Mr. Pink-Whistle. "One will burst and make a very horrible smell. One will mew like a cat. One will cluck like a hen, and the last one will grow tiny legs and run all over Mr. Smarmy."

Sooty giggled, and when a cat giggles it sounds very funny indeed. "I wish I was going to see all that," said Sooty.

"Well, I'm going to!" said Mr. Pink-Whistle. "I want to see Mr. Smarmy taught a lesson. It's quite time he was!"

Now, Mr. Smarmy, after he had taken the eggs, went to his sister Lucy's for breakfast. He didn't give her any of the eggs. Oh, no! He was going to take those home, after he had done his work that day, and ask his wife to make a nice fat omelette for him.

"I've got a busy day, Lucy," he said. "Got to see a lot of important people. Mustn't be late at the office. The first meeting is at half-past nine."

Mr. Smarmy arrived there at just before half-past nine. But he couldn't take any of the eggs out of his pockets because two of the men he was going to meet had already arrived.

"Good morning!" said Mr. Smarmy. "Nice and early! Aha! Here are the others, too!"

Soon seven men were sitting down round the table—and an eighth, who could not be seen, was standing opposite Mr. Smarmy. That was Mr. Pink-Whistle, of course, who had made himself invisible, and was at the meeting unknown to anyone.

The meeting began. Mr. Smarmy wanted to ask the six men round him to lend him money for his business, so he was very polite indeed. Everyone listened to him quietly — till the first egg went POP.

"POP!" It burst with a loud noise, rather like a paper bag when it is blown up and goes bang. Everyone jumped and looked at Mr. Smarmy. He looked alarmed. "What was that?" he said.

"It sounded as if it came from somewhere about you," said one man. "Good gracious, look! What's that mess trickling out of one of your pockets? Looks like egg!"

It *was* egg, of course. Mr. Smarmy looked down in disgust at the yellow mess that was seeping out of his pocket. How horrible! That egg must have been bad, to blow up like that!

He tried to wipe the mess away with his clean handkerchief. Then another egg began its magic work. It mewed like a cat!

"Mew-ew-ew-ew! Mew-ew-ew-ew!"

"There's a cat somewhere," said one of the men. "Sounds as if you've got it on your knee, Mr. Smarmy."

160

"Mew-ew-ew-ew!" Mr. Smarmy jumped up in alarm, for the noise came from somewhere about him, there was no doubt of that. And then the mewing egg went off with a pop just as the other one had done!

Everyone jumped at the POP, and stared at another yellow mess coming from a pocket the other side of Mr. Smarmy's coat. "Is this some kind of a joke?" asked a man.

"No — no! I assure you I can't imagine *what* is happening!" said poor Mr. Smarmy. "Oh, dear — there goes another one!"

"POP!" Another egg burst, and this time there was such a terrible smell that everyone got out their handkerchiefs at once. "Pooh," said one of the men. "Smarmy, do you often carry bad eggs about? I hope you are not a bad egg yourself! Pooh! What a fearful smell."

Mr. Smarmy was most distressed. This meeting was not going at all well. Blow those eggs! He wished he hadn't taken

162

them that morning. They must all be bad ones. He heard a little chuckle close to his ear and turned in alarm.

It was Mr. Pink-Whistle, but, of course, Mr. Smarmy couldn't see him. Pink-Whistle was having a lovely time. What a joke! It was nice to see a horrid person like Mr. Smarmy getting into trouble like this.

The meeting went on again, after Mr. Smarmy had tried to clean himself up. And then the fourth egg began to cluck like a hen. It went off very loudly indeed.

"Cuck-cuck-cuck-cuck-cuck! Cuck-cuck-cuck-cuck-cuck! CUCK-CUCK!"

"Good gracious! He's got a hen in his pocket now!" cried one of the men. "Smarmy, what is the meaning of this? Is this the way to get us to lend money to you — to play idiotic tricks of this kind?"

"Sir, I assure you — —" began poor Mr. Smarmy, clutching in alarm at the egg that was clucking, but before he could finish it went POP, too! And then there was another yellow mess to clear up!

"Do you always carry bad eggs about with you?" asked one of the men. "Have you any more? If so, I advise you to remove them from your pockets, Smarmy. We've had enough of eggs this morning."

"There's one more," said poor Smarmy, putting his hand into a pocket. "I'll take it out. Oh—it's running away from me! Oh, it's gone down my trouser leg! Now it's running up again! It's inside my vest. It's tickling me. It's got legs, I'm sure!"

All the men stared at Mr. Smarmy in amazement. The egg had grown legs, just as Pink-Whistle had said it would, and was running about all over him. He kept clutching at it, but it always slipped away somewhere else.

"He's mad!" said one of the men, getting up. "Well, I didn't come here to have egg-tricks played on me. I'm not putting any money into a business run by a man who plays silly conjuring tricks with eggs that pop and mew and cluck and grow legs. Not I!"

"Nor I!" cried all the others, and they

got up to go. Mr. Smarmy stared at them in dismay. "Please, please wait!" he cried. "This is the last egg. Do wait!"

POP! The last egg burst, too—and that was enough for the men. They went out of the room, talking loudly about people who seemed to think it was funny to play tricks with bad eggs. Mr. Smarmy was left alone, with a burst egg trickling down his leg.

He groaned. Then he felt a tap on his shoulder. He looked up in surprise, to see Mr. Pink-Whistle looking sternly down at him. It made Mr. Smarmy jump to see him there so suddenly.

"This is what happens to people who steal eggs from a little girl's hens," said Mr. Pink-Whistle. "Bad things always come from bad deeds. None of those men will lend you the money you want. It serves you right."

Mr. Smarmy groaned again and buried his face in his hands. "It does, I know it does," he said. "I'm a deceitful fellow. I pretend to be so good—and yet I am mean enough to take eggs belonging to a little girl's hens. I deserve all this. I don't know who you are, or how you know about it, or why those eggs behaved like that—I only know I'm ashamed and sorry."

"That's good," said Mr. Pink-Whistle, pleased. "Very good. What about buying a beautiful doll for the little girl, and

166

putting it in the hen-house for her to find to-morrow, to make up for the eggs you took, Mr. Smarmy? And what about trying to be as good and proper as you are always pretending to be? If you are really sorry, you can do that, too."

And then away went Mr. Pink-Whistle to tell Sooty all that had happened. But you may be sure he will be hiding, unseen, in the hen-house on the morning when there is a beautiful new doll waiting for Annabelle. She will be so surprised and pleased—and dear old Pink-Whistle wants to see her happy face.

He really is a kind old thing, isn't he?

XI

MR. PINK-WHISTLE GOES TO SCHOOL

Mr. Pink-Whistle was walking down the road wondering if the fishmonger had any kippers for himself and Sooty, his cat, when four girls and two boys came running along.

"Quick!" said one. "Get round the corner before Harry and George see us!"

They shot round the corner—and then came the sound of pattering footsteps behind Mr. Pink-Whistle once more, and along came two big boys, almost knocking him over.

Mr. Pink-Whistle went spinning into the gutter and just saved himself from sitting down hard by clutching at a lamppost.

The two boys didn't say they were sorry, they didn't even stop! They rushed round the corner after the smaller children.

"Good gracious!" said Mr. Pink-Whistle, letting go the lamp-post. "What unpleasant boys! Who are they, I wonder?"

He went round the corner. He saw Harry and George pouncing on the smaller children and taking their hats and caps away. They sent them sailing up into the trees and over the hedges!

"You are hateful," said a small girl,

beginning to cry. "You're always playing horrid tricks, and making us take the blame!"

"You hid my French book yesterday and I got into trouble for it," said Joan.

"You spilt my ink-pot all over the floor, and I had to stay in," said Peter. "I know you did it! It's just the kind of thing you always do."

"Yes—and then you leave us to bear the blame," said Doris. "And if we tell tales of you you smack our faces and tramp on our toes!"

Harry pounced on Doris and pulled her hair so hard that she squealed.

"Let go!" she said.

Mr. Pink-Whistle made himself invisible. He crept up to Harry, caught hold of his hair and tugged hard.

"Oh!" said Harry, and swung round. George was just near by. "Did you pull my hair? What do you think you're doing?"

"I didn't touch you," said George. "Don't be silly!"

Then the two boys glared at one another

and put up their fists to fight. The other children saw their chance and ran off at once. Let them fight! They wouldn't bother the others then!

Mr. Pink-Whistle didn't like the two boys at all. He took a look at them. Their faces were hard. It wouldn't be any good talking to them, or pleading with them to be better. They would laugh.

"No — the only thing is to do the same things to them that they do to others," decided Mr. Pink-Whistle. "I shall go to school with these children this afternoon. Ha — there'll be a bit of fun then! But not for George or Harry!"

He waited for the children that afternoon and then walked along beside them, unseen. He saw how they all ran away from George and Harry, and how frightened of the two big boys they were.

"A couple of bullies!" said Mr. Pink-Whistle. "Well, well — bullies are always cowards, so we'll just see what Harry and George do when unpleasant things begin to happen to them. They shall take the blame for things I do this afternoon, in return for making others take the blame for things that they so often have done."

He went into the schoolroom with Harry and George and the rest of their class. He noticed where the two big boys sat and went over to them. Nobody could see him. He was quite invisible, of course.

When George was bending down to pick up a dropped pencil Mr. Pink-Whistle opened his desk lid and let it drop with a terrific BANG!

Everyone jumped. The teacher frowned. "George! There's no need to make that noise."

"I didn't," said George, indignantly. "I was bending down. Someone else must have banged my desk-lid."

"Was it you, Harry?" asked the teacher. Harry always sat next to George.

"No, it wasn't," said Harry, rudely.

Well, Mr. Pink-Whistle managed to bang George's desk-lid twice more, and the teacher began to blame Harry, because George was so very indignant that she felt sure it couldn't be his fault.

The two boys glared at one another. Then Mr. Pink-Whistle tipped a pile of books off Harry's desk when he wasn't looking!

"HARRY!" said the teacher.

"I didn't do it," said Harry, angrily. "Make George pick up my books. He must have done that."

"I didn't," said George. "Yah!"

"Boys, boys!" said the teacher. "George, come up here and write on the board for me. Write down the home-work notes for to-morrow."

George went up sulkily. He took up the chalk and began to write on the board. Mr. Pink-Whistle was just behind him, invisible.

He took George's hand and began to guide the piece of chalk. And do you know what he wrote? He wrote this:

"Harry is a silly donkey. Harry is a dunce. Harry is . . ."

George was horrified. Whatever was the chalk doing? It seemed to be writing by itself, and he couldn't stop it. And look what it was writing too! Whatever would his teacher say? Where was the duster? He must rub out the rude writing at once!

Aha! Mr. Pink-Whistle had taken the duster, of course. He had thrown it up to the top of a picture. George couldn't see it anywhere.

The children saw what George had written, and they began to nudge one another and giggle. The teacher turned to see what George was doing behind her — and dear me, she saw what he had written on the blackboard!

"GEORGE!" she said angrily. "How dare you do that? What in the world are you thinking of? Rub it out at once."

"I didn't mean to," said poor George. "It felt as if the chalk was writing by itself."

"Oh, don't be so silly," said the teacher. "My goodness me — look where the duster has been thrown to! Did you throw it there, George? You'd better lose ten marks straight away for your silly behaviour this afternoon!"

Harry laughed like anything. He was angry with George for writing rude things about him on the board. Mr. Pink-Whistle waited till George was back in his seat and then he pulled Harry's hair quite hard.

Harry jumped and glared round at George. Mr. Pink-Whistle tugged at George's hair then. George jumped and glared round at Harry.

"Stop that!" they said to each other, and the teacher banged on her desk for quiet.

Well, Mr. Pink-Whistle quite enjoyed himself that afternoon and so did all the class, except Harry and George. Harry's ruler shot off his desk. George's pencil-box upset all over the floor. Harry's shoe-laces came mysteriously undone three times. George's socks kept slipping down to his ankles, and his jersey buttons came undone at his neck. It was all very extra-ordinary.

They all went out to play for ten minutes. Mr. Pink-Whistle went with them. He kicked Harry's ball into the next-door garden. He tripped George up twice and sent him rolling over and over. The two boys got very angry indeed, because they both felt certain it was the other one playing tricks.

After a few minutes Mr. Pink-Whistle went indoors. He went to Harry's desk and put half his books into George's. He put

George's pencils into Harry's box. That was the kind of thing the two boys were always doing to other people. Well, let them see if they liked it or not!

They didn't like it a bit. Harry wailed aloud when he found half his books gone, because the teacher was always very cross when anyone was careless with books. And George was furious to find his best pencils missing.

"Who's taken them? Wait till I find out!" he cried angrily. "Teacher—all my best pencils have gone!"

They were found in Harry's box almost at once, and George almost flew at him in rage. He would have hit him then and there if the teacher hadn't suddenly discovered that Harry's books were in George's desk! She was really disgusted.

"I thought you two boys were friends. Look at this—your books in George's desk, Harry, and all George's pencils in your box. You ought to be ashamed of yourselves. Any more nonsense from either of you and you will stay in for half an hour."

Well, there was quite a lot of nonsense of course—but it was from Mr. Pink-Whistle, not from the boys! He upset George's paint-pot all over his painting —a thing that George himself did to somebody almost every painting lesson! And he smudged Harry's best writing when he wasn't looking. And that, too, was something that Harry was very fond of doing

178

to the smaller children.

The teacher was cross. "Stay in for half an hour, both of you," she said. "I don't care if you *are* going out to a party. You can be half an hour late."

"But you *know* it's my cousin's birthday party," said George, indignantly. "I *can't* be late."

"I know all about the party — and I'm afraid you *will* be late, both of you!" said the teacher, firmly. The two boys glared at one another. Each felt sure it was the other who had got him into all this trouble!

They had to stay in for half an hour and do most of their work again. Then they said a sulky good-bye and went out.

As soon as they got out in the road they began to quarrel. "I suppose you think you were very clever this afternoon!" said George, angrily. "Well, take *that*!"

And he hit Harry hard on the back. Mr. Pink-Whistle grinned. A fight? Well, he would join in as well. He would repay both George and Harry the smacks and slaps and biffs and thuds that they had many a time dealt out to the younger children.

So, quite invisible, he hopped in and out, dealing a slap here and a smack there, and making the boys yell in pain, and go for each other all the more.

Biff! That was George hitting Harry on the nose. It began to bleed.

Smack! That was Harry hitting George on his right eye. It began to go black at once.

Thud, bang, slap! That was Mr. Pink-Whistle doing his share!

BIFF-BANG! That was both boys at once—and they fell over, crash, into a muddy puddle. They sat up, howling.

"Let's stop," wept George. "My eye hurts. And your nose is bleeding. We're terribly late for the party. We shall miss all the good things at tea."

So, sniffing and snuffling, muddy, wet and very much the worse for wear, the two boys arrived at their cousin's house. But when their aunt saw them, she was very cross indeed.

"George! Harry! How *can* you come to a party looking like that? Have you been fighting one another? You should be ashamed of yourselves. One with a black eye and one with a bleeding nose! And so dirty and untidy too. I won't let you in. You shan't come to the party!"

And she slammed the door in their faces.

They went howling down the street, very sorry for themselves.

Mr. Pink-Whistle began to think they might have learnt their lesson. He suddenly appeared beside them, a kind little man with pointed ears.

"Come and have tea with me," he said. "I live not far off with my cat Sooty."

So they went with him, still sniffing. He made them wash and brush their hair. He stopped Harry's nose from bleeding, and he bathed George's eye. Then he sat them down to bread and butter and honey and a seed-cake.

"You're very kind," said George, surprised.

"I'm not always," said Mr. Pink-Whistle, solemnly. "Sometimes, when I see mean, unkind people I get that way myself — just to punish them, you know. I've had a good time this afternoon, punishing two nasty little boys. My word, they were horrid little things — always teasing the smaller ones and getting them into trouble."

The two boys gazed at him, afraid.

"You've no idea of the things I did!" said Mr. Pink-Whistle, passing them the seed-cake. "My, the tricks I played in their class this afternoon—and what a time I had when those boys fought. I fought, too—biff, bang, thud!"

The boys looked at one another uncomfortably. They both felt very scared.

"You know, I always think that if mean, unkind people get treated meanly and unkindly themselves sometimes, they learn how horrid it is," said Mr. Pink-Whistle. "Of course—they sometimes need more than one lesson—perhaps two, or four, or even six!"

He looked hard at the two boys. They looked back. "Sir," said George, in a small voice. "We shan't need more than that one lesson. I promise you that."

"I promise you, too," said Harry, in a whisper. "It's—it's very kind of you, sir, to take us home and give us this tea—when you know we're mean."

"Bless us all, you can come again as

183

often as you like — so long as you don't need another lesson from me, but only a nice tea!" said kind Mr. Pink-Whistle. "Now do take another piece of cake each — just to show there's no ill-feeling between us!"

Well, they did, of course. And, so far as I know, Mr. Pink-Whistle hasn't had to give them another lesson — yet! But he would, you know, if they broke their promise. He's kind — but he's fierce, too, when he's putting wrong things right!

THE END

The first book about
Mr. Pink-Whistle
is
THE ADVENTURES OF MR. PINK-WHISTLE

Also by Enid Blyton

THE ADVENTURES OF
MR PINK-WHISTLE

"I've got a secret!" whispered Mr Pink-Whistle. "I can make myself invisible whenever I like!"

Mr Pink-Whistle is half man and half brownie. He has magic green eyes and magic powers – like making himself invisible. He hates anything unfair or unkind so with the help of his magic he goes about putting wrong things right.

Enid Blyton

THE ENCHANTED WOOD

"Up the Faraway Tree,
Jo, Bessie and me!"

Jo, Bessie and Fanny move to the country
and find an Enchanted Wood right on their
doorstep! And in the wood stands the magic
Faraway Tree where the Saucepan Man,
Moon-Face and Silky the elf live. Together
they visit the strange lands which lie at the
top of the tree, and have the most exciting
adventures – and narrow escapes.

More magical stories can be found in

The Magic Faraway Tree
The Folk of the Faraway Tree

Enid Blyton

MR MEDDLE'S MISCHIEF

"You're a tiresome, meddlesome creature, Mister Meddle!"

Mr Meddle is a very silly pixie. He's always getting in a muddle. He washes his hair with sherbet and cleans his teeth with glue; he feeds cakes mixture to the pigs and worms to the budgies; he meddles with a conjuror's magic and drives an engine into the river. He just can't keep out of trouble!

You can have more fun with Mr Meddle in *Mr Meddle's Muddles*.

Enid Blyton

MR MEDDLE'S MUDDLES

"Will you keep away from me?" roared Meddle, getting angry. "You're a most annoying dream."

Mr Meddle can't do anything right. He's always getting into trouble, especially when he tries his best to be helpful. In these muddlesome stories, he throws away Aunt Jemima's luggage, has a fight with a kangaroo and is chased by an angry bull!

You can have more fun with Mr Meddle in *Mr Meddle's Mischief*.

Enid Blyton

THE SEASIDE FAMILY

They were off – off to Sea-gull Cove by the sea!

Mike, Belinda and Ann are going on a seaside holiday. What's more, they are taking their home with them – it's easy when you live in a caravan! And what a wonderful summer lies ahead, with the sea right outside their door!

Enid Blyton

THE SAUCY JANE FAMILY

"Welcome to the Saucy Jane!"

Mike, Belinda and Ann spend their holidays on a beautiful houseboat on the canal – and what an exciting time they have! They learn to swim and have some wonderful holiday treats – like taking a trip on a real canal boat.

A Selected List of Fiction from Mammoth

While every effort is made to keep prices low, it is sometimes necessary to increase prices at short notice. Mammoth Books reserves the right to show new retail prices on covers which may differ from those previously advertised in the text or elsewhere.

The prices shown below were correct at the time of going to press.

☐	416 13972 8	**Why the Whales Came**	Michael Morpurgo	£2.50
☐	7497 0034 3	**My Friend Walter**	Michael Morpurgo	£2.50
☐	7497 0035 1	**The Animals of Farthing Wood**	Colin Dann	£2.99
☐	7497 0136 6	**I Am David**	Anne Holm	£2.50
☐	7497 0139 0	**Snow Spider**	Jenny Nimmo	£2.50
☐	7497 0140 4	**Emlyn's Moon**	Jenny Nimmo	£2.25
☐	7497 0344 X	**The Haunting**	Margaret Mahy	£2.25
☐	416 96850 3	**Catalogue of the Universe**	Margaret Mahy	£1.95
☐	7497 0051 3	**My Friend Flicka**	Mary O'Hara	£2.99
☐	7497 0079 3	**Thunderhead**	Mary O'Hara	£2.99
☐	7497 0219 2	**Green Grass of Wyoming**	Mary O'Hara	£2.99
☐	416 13722 9	**Rival Games**	Michael Hardcastle	£1.99
☐	416 13212 X	**Mascot**	Michael Hardcastle	£1.99
☐	7497 0126 9	**Half a Team**	Michael Hardcastle	£1.99
☐	416 08812 0	**The Whipping Boy**	Sid Fleischman	£1.99
☐	7497 0033 5	**The Lives of Christopher Chant**	Diana Wynne-Jones	£2.50
☐	7497 0164 1	**A Visit to Folly Castle**	Nina Beachcroft	£2.25

All these books are available at your bookshop or newsagent, or can be ordered direct from the publisher. Just tick the titles you want and fill in the form below.

Mandarin Paperbacks, Cash Sales Department, PO Box 11, Falmouth, Cornwall TR10 9EN.

Please send cheque or postal order, no currency, for purchase price quoted and allow the following for postage and packing:

UK	80p for the first book, 20p for each additional book ordered to a maximum charge of £2.00.
BFPO	80p for the first book, 20p for each additional book.
Overseas including Eire	£1.50 for the first book, £1.00 for the second and 30p for each additional book thereafter.

NAME (Block letters) ....

ADDRESS ....

....

....